KILTY

AS

CHARGED

KILTY SERIES: BOOK ONE

Amy Vansant

Dedication

To my husband, who blurted out the title of this book and made me want to write a whole novel for it.

INTRODUCTION

"...the mysterious man known only as Ryft worked at Rob Roy MacGregor's side, serving as his preternatural shadow; a swift hand of justice so inescapable that the MacGregor's enemies grew to fear him greater than any other man in the Highlands. The loathing that Thorn Campbell, leader of a mercenary clan known as the Rùn, had for the paladin grew so malevolent that the land itself roiled beneath the relentless tread of his obsession.

Unable to assassinate his enemy, Thorn challenged Ryft to final combat in the fields of Glen Orchy.

His provocation proved a ruse.

Even as the men prepared to meet, word came to Ryft that his beloved wife, Isobel, and infant son, had been burned to death in their home by Thorn's men.

The Highland people still tell the tale of the fearsome battle that ensued between the two mortal enemies and of how a mysterious fog engulfed the men as they clashed, until only the sounds of swords biting metal and flesh echoed across the field of conflict.

When the fog lifted, the men were gone, two swords the only remnants of the reckoning. Ryft's weapon stood buried to the hilt in the Highland soil. Thorn's lay flat beside it, forsaken.

Some say Ryft's love for his wife had been so great that he'd sent Thorn to hell and then gone with him, just to be sure he'd stay."

--- Ancient Highland Folklore

CHAPTER ONE

Catriona found the body on Stage Fourteen of Parasol Pictures—lying over a barrel like a dead cowboy draped across a horse bound for home.

She scowled. The figure's plaid skirt was hiked high enough that she could see the curve of buttocks, even in the dim light of the closed studio.

Those buttocks drew her attention like a train wreck.

The thighs were *hairy*.

A pig snort ripped through the room, and the body spasmed.

Catriona relaxed a notch.

Snoring. Not dead...

"Hey—Sleeping Beauty."

She poked the body with the tip of her boot. It felt *solid*.

"Wow. What have they been feeding *you*?"

She assumed she'd stumbled onto some sort of weightlifting chick, who, by the smell of her, recently backstroked in a tank of Scotch.

Or...*No.* She reconsidered. The dim light played tricks on her eyes. It wasn't a skirt at all, crumpled on that firm gluteus maximus like a wadded plaid tissue.

It was a *kilt*.

Sleeping Beauty is a man.

She sighed. It wasn't unusual to find drunks on a Hollywood

set. The guy was likely background talent from some Highland romance. She didn't know of any such films in production, but Highlanders had picked up where vampires left off. It wasn't hard to imagine another Scottish love story under development. The guy probably wrapped his first day of shooting, felt the need to celebrate with some of the more seasoned cast, and over imbibed. Experienced talent *loved* to make the newbies suffer.

Catriona liked to think rolling drunks off the lot was beneath her, but as Parasol Picture's studio "fixer," nothing was *officially* beneath her. She spent her days scurrying male leads from their leading ladies' trailers moments before their wives arrived for surprise visits, sneaking stars in and out of rehab, quelling rivalries, and rousing sleeping drunks before they destroyed filming schedules.

Corralling spoiled Hollywood elite before they cost the studio money or reputation was rarely as glamorous as it sounded. Shoving drunken background talent into a cab wasn't the most unseemly thing she'd ever done.

Not even *close*.

She eyed the sleeping man's tush and raised her hand.

Speaking of background talent—

Crack! She slapped the exposed buttcheek with a satisfying echo and surprised herself by giggling.

That was way too much fun.

"Eh?" The man's head lifted a few inches, revealing sex-confirming chin stubble.

Clearing her throat, Catriona adopted a disapproving frown. "You know, you *can* wear underwear beneath a kilt. You don't *have* to be so authentic."

The man's head fell, and his breathing grew heavy once more.

She tapped him with her toe. "Hey. Come on. You can't sleep here, buddy. Time to go home."

He flapped his hand in her direction. "Away with ye, wummin."

Catriona scowled. "All right. Cameras are off, Mr. Connery. Time to go home. You can drop the Highlander crap."

She tugged on his kilt, and he slid from the barrel and onto his back. Through some miracle, the kilt kept his twigs and berries covered throughout the process.

Perhaps he'd been hired for that very talent.

"Hey—Braveheart. You have to go *home*."

"Home? Noo?" His forearm flopped across his face. He sounded more like a braying moose than a man; as if he were saying *now* and trying to swallow his tongue at the same time.

"*Home. Now.* You know, where you hang your skirt. You can't sleep here."

She kicked his bare thigh, and he sat up like a spring-loaded vampire. Startled by his sudden movement, she stumbled back against an adjacent barrel. A mop of scraggly, dark hair bounced from the man's face, revealing a strong jawline, full lips, and an angry scar that ran from his temple to his cheekbone.

With great effort, he opened an eye in her direction, but Catriona felt confident he couldn't focus. Blue irises swam in his bloodshot eyeballs like fish in a bowl. His pupils did a few laps and then rolled back into his head as he collapsed once more.

Catriona tilted her head back and sighed.

Grabbing his arm, she jerked him back to a sitting position, but her best efforts at hauling him to his feet only listed him to the left.

Seriously?

Shifting, she clutched him by the front of his loose-fitting white shirt and tugged. She almost had him sitting when the fabric gave way, and he flopped back to the ground.

His head smacked the cement floor with an angry thud. She winced.

Whoops.

The man's newly naked pecs looked like flesh-colored dinner plates.

Dinner plates with nipples.

Casting had outdone themselves, finding such a beefcake to swing swords around in the background of the fighting scenes. It made Catriona wonder if he was *someone*, maybe playing the lead's brother or best friend?

Nah. She made it a point to know everyone on the lot who was *someone.* This guy was no one. A fine specimen of *nobody.* Hotties with gym memberships scurried around the lot like ants daily. Most couldn't pull their IQs out of double digits if they pooled their resources.

Still—she put her hand on his left pec and let it slide along the curve.

"Wake up," she whispered, trying to fool both him and herself she was trying to rouse him and *not* copping a cheap feel.

Hm. My my.

She patted his chest with her fingertips—once to say *back to business!* and then twice because she appreciated the spring of it.

I really need to start dating again.

Standing, she put her hands on her hips and glared down at him. His mouth had fallen open to better facilitate his snoring.

Now what? The guy was *out* and weighed as much as a water buffalo.

She spotted a dolly and rolled it to him. Shimmying it beneath his legs, she used every last bit of strength to heft his hips onto the platform. Panting, she collapsed beside it, his torso and head still twisted at an unnatural angle on the ground. After a short rest, she shoved the rest of him on board. She had to shift him to get his body secured, but his legs, now dragging on the ground like a fish tail, made it difficult to push him.

There is just no reason to make a body this big.

Walking to the opposite end of the dolly, she lifted his feet and split them on either side of her. His skirt began to slip, and she dropped his legs.

Oh! Whoa! No. Bad idea.

She set down his legs and adjusted his kilt.

With a huff, she rolled him on his side, hoping to curl him into a more compact fetal position. It worked for a moment, but as soon as she tried to roll the dolly, his legs uncurled like a flower opening to the morning sun, and they again dragged across the ground.

She huffed.

For the love of Diana Gabaldon—

With great difficulty, she rolled him on his stomach and, grabbing a thin extension cord, tied his ankles together. She folded him at the knees and wrapped the other end of the cord to the front wheelbase, hogtying him to the dolly. When his arms flopped off the sides, she untied the cord from the front, wrapped it around his wrists, and then retied it.

"Look here, I caught me a man," she said, clapping her hands together. She rolled him out of the building, pleased with her ingenuity.

Outside and out of breath, she straightened and stared up at the moon.

What to do?

She couldn't dump an unconscious man into a cab: she didn't know where to send it.

She pushed her trophy several buildings away to the office, over which she lived in a third-floor apartment, and, after cresting the door entry, rolled him into the elevator. She propelled him down the short hallway to her door and, with a shove of her boot, pushed the snoring lump inside her apartment. He glided across the stained cement floor like a ballerina on a skateboard, hogtied and drooling.

Untying his arms and legs, she attempted to move him to the sofa before abandoning the idea. After considering her options, she left him on his side on the dolly. She feared, on his back, he'd choke should he become sick during the night, and leaving him face down didn't seem right. Nobody wanted to wake up with rug impressions all over their face. She'd figured that out the hard way a long time ago.

She shook a finger at him. "Don't barf on my rug."

Feeling she'd done all she could, she retired to her bedroom.

A few minutes later, she popped her head out the door and taped a note to it.

> *Don't even think about coming in here. There are cameras everywhere, I am a light sleeper, and I own several guns.*

She read it and nodded.

That ought to do it.

Retreating once more, she locked the door.

She made it halfway through brushing her teeth before returning to the living room to scrawl an addendum to her note.

> *I am an MMA fighter named Tank. I was forced to retire after accidentally killing a man.*

She returned to the bedroom, changed into an oversized tee, and unlocked the door one last time.

> *PS: It wasn't an accident.*

CHAPTER TWO

Forty Years Ago

The lights sped by him until he felt *mad*. His head swam. When he spotted the well-lit building and the figures of men and women eating inside, he yelped with joy.

Food.

That, he understood. The building was strange, but it had to be some kind of pub. A pint would help him gather his thoughts.

Thorn entered through a glass door. The lights above were blinding—he squinted at them through his fingers—giant squares of bright light, as if someone had boxed the sun and installed it in the ceiling.

He lowered his arm and found it covered in cuts and dried blood.

"Just come from the studio?" said a voice.

He turned to find a heavyset woman wearing what looked like her shift, staring at him, her jaw working as if she was chewing cud.

"Eh?"

"That outfit of yours. You a movie star?"

A man sitting at the window snickered.

Thorn turned on him, his fist raised. "Roar again 'n' ye'll cop th' back o' mah hand."

The man's smile vanished. His gaze darted away.

A pain shot through Thorn's skull, and he groaned. He peered at the woman with one eye closed. "Git me a whisky, wifie."

"Listen to the accent on you. Don't have a liquor license here, sweetie, but I can get you a coffee. That work?"

The world began to spin, and Thorn took a seat on a strange high stool tucked up against a tall bartop.

"Aye," was all he could manage to say.

The woman disappeared, and he dropped his head in his hands.

Where am I?

He couldn't remember anything, but he was certain this wasn't a place he knew. Everything was too shiny and smooth. *Everything was wrong.*

A large man appeared at his arm. "Heya, buddy," he said, sitting beside Thorn, his rump nearly too large to fit on the stool. He wore a shirt in a plaid pattern Thorn found comforting.

"Tracy, get me one of those roast beefs to go, will you?"

The woman in the shift put a mug of dark liquid in front of Thorn and nodded before disappearing into the back.

Thorn focused on the man beside him. It helped him keep his balance. "Where am ah?"

The man grinned. "This is the Triple-T Diner. Or did you mean the city? Los Angeles? Nah. I can tell by that crazy fake blood on your face that you know you're in L.A. Let me guess; you're playing *dead guy number two*? Am I right?" He laughed as if he'd told a joke.

Thorn felt his face and dried blood flaked into his lap, darkening his already muddy breeches. The sleeve of his jacket was torn. The memory of a dark-skinned man tossing him out of the fenced area where he'd awoken flashed before his eyes.

His new friend at the Triple-T Diner wore blue trousers made from what looked like a thick, durable fabric. He'd seen similar trews on several other men and more than one woman since arriving in this godforsaken place.

I should kill him and take those. Help me fit in with this crowd...

Oblivious to Thorn's thoughts, the man jabbered on. "This is a good diner, I'll tell you that, and I've been to 'em *all*. Thought I'd stop in and get some grub for the drive. Headin' back to Campbell County, you know. Take a couple days, so I'll be stopping in a lot more diners, yessir."

Thorn's interest perked. "Campbell County?"

"Yep. Campbell County, Tennessee. That's where I hang my hat. I drive a semi. Got some side businesses, though, back home." He winked. "Where do you hail from?"

Thorn heard the word leave his mouth before considering the question. "Glenorchy."

"Never heard of it. This *Glen-Nokee* near here?"

Thorn looked around the strange room.

"No."

Of that, he was fairly certain.

"You passing through? Or trying to get famous?"

"Aye. No." Thorn's left eye began to twitch, and he put his hand on it, hoping to keep it still. The man's questions were making less and less sense to him. A relentless pain throbbed in his head.

"Hey, let me throw something out here," said the man. "I had a guy pull out on me at the last second. I saw how you handled chuckles over there, and I like the cut of your jib. And, *bonus*, you're a big boy, like me. You're just the kinda guy I need in my line of work." He leaned forward to peer into Thorn's face. "I don't suppose you're looking for honest work?"

Thorn traced his finger across the countertop as he pieced together the man's request.

Nae. None of it made sense.

"I dinnae ken," he muttered.

The man shrugged. "I'll take that to mean you're open to the idea. See, I'm starting a new enterprise back home, and I need boys like you to protect my business. I knew you'd be interested. Or, do you want to spend the rest of your life wearing *pantaloons* or whatever you call that crazy getup?"

Thorn considered the offer. He had no idea where he might go after he left the Triple-T Diner.

"Ye'll take me to County Campbell?" he asked.

"Campbell County. You bet. Hey, I just realized we haven't even been properly introduced. I'm Dave. Dave Brown." He held out a large paw.

Thorn shook his hand. "Thorn Campbell."

The man's expression lit. "You're kidding. Your last name is *Campbell*?"

"Aye."

"This was meant to be. I'll tell you what, though, I can't wait around. You got a car?"

"Ah—no?"

"No? Well, I can take you somewhere to grab your stuff, but then we got to get on the road. Where you living?"

Thorn shook his head. "Nowhere."

The man cocked an eyebrow and poked at the ground. "You want to leave right from here?"

Thorn nodded. "Ah do."

"Well, *all right*." He slapped Thorn on the back, and the Highlander's fingers curled into a fist before he could stop them.

Dave laughed.

"Tough guy. Man, I *like* you. This was fate, Thorn, I'm telling you, *fate*."

CHAPTER THREE

He awoke with a snort.

When he sat up, the world wobbled. He thrust out both hands to his sides to steady himself, only to find the floor several inches lower than his body.

Am ah floating?

His shirt fell open, the buttons having been torn away, and he spent a minute forlornly staring at his belly button, head throbbing to the beat of his heart.

He growled, fingering the torn white fabric hanging from his torso.

I hate mending shirts.

Rubbing one eye, he surveyed his surroundings with the other. The walls of the room were smooth and white. Gray cabinets lined the far wall, interspersed with shiny silver boxes of various sizes, one nearly as large as himself. It looked like a coffin.

Funny way to sit a coffin, upended, no matter how fancy it might be.

It had the man's name on it, though.

'Frigidaire.'

Sounds French.

He shifted, and the dolly beneath him slid away, dumping him on the cold floor. He worked his tongue against the roof of his mouth, recognizing the familiar taste of whisky combined with what felt like a sheep's hide.

Light glowed from outside a pair of windows. He stood to shuffle over and investigate, every movement aching his muscles. His mind roiled with fog.

The light outside didn't shine from a full moon but a powerful candle sitting high on a stick. The moon-on-a-stick revealed a row of plain square buildings as if he were in a village—though no village he'd ever seen.

Everything was so strange.

I must be in France.

Wincing, he stretched his back and felt a pain grab near his hip. He unbelted and dropped his kilt to reveal a cut, deep but not dire, situated above his hip bone. The dried blood on the wound pulled at his flesh when he moved. Licking his fingers, he rubbed at it before noticing an indentation in the wall.

A *door.*

At least it *appeared* to be a door. Instead of a latch, the door had a silver metal orb stuck to the front of it, where a latch might be. He wrapped his fingers around it and pulled, pushed, and turned. Turning felt most right; it gave but ultimately thwarted him.

Locked.

He took a step back and braced himself to run his shoulder at it. Squaring up to the door, his gaze floated upward, and he noticed a window over the door. His head lolled to the side as he considered this.

Best take a peek before I pound my way into a fight.

Jumping, he caught the sill and pulled himself up to peer through the window.

A girl on a bed.

She didn't appear dangerous. She wore only a short, tight shift, her bare legs spread akimbo as if she'd been dropped there from a great height. From what he could see, she was bonny indeed. Dark hair framed high cheekbones and a straight, dainty nose. Her lips were plump with a hint of pink color. Beneath her shift, he could see the curve of her—

He dropped to the ground and ran a hand through his hair.

He felt flush.

Had he been with the girl and then locked himself out somehow?

No. I'd mind such an odd place...and such a bonny lassie.

He raised his hand to knock and then reconsidered. She'd appeared peaceful. Maybe he'd better get a lay of the land.

He noticed a note on the ground in front of the door. He picked it up and held it near the window to read it.

Although his mothers had taught him to be an *excellent* reader, some of the words on the note didn't make sense. He had no idea what an *MMA fighter* was, though it worried him the mysterious lass felt a need to declare her affiliation to such a violent clan so soon after meeting him. From what he could piece together, she didn't want him coming into her room, and she was a known killer in possession of a firearm.

He grinned. He couldn't remember much, but she felt like his kind of lassie.

Looking down, his amusement faded.

Hm.

Maybe I should put my clothes back on before she comes out here and shoots me dead.

Taking a stride toward his discarded kilt, the room swam before his eyes.

"Keep the heid," he muttered, a phrase he often used to calm himself. He'd been told it was his father's favorite saying, though the man died when he was only a wee thing.

Throwing out a hand, he hoped to use a wall to steady himself but found no wall within reach. He stumbled toward the long soft chair...

Maybe one more wee nap...

CHAPTER FOUR

At the sound of the *bang!* Catriona sat straight up in bed and shot her hand beneath her pillow to find her gun. Holding her breath, she listened for the source of the rude awakening.

Sleeping on a Hollywood studio lot, it wasn't unusual to hear strange sounds in the middle of the night. Carousing actors, dinosaur roars, laser fights, screeching demons... she'd heard it all. A *bang* was pretty ho-hum. But something about this bang—

Thud! Thududud...

There it was again.

Someone's in my apartment.

Catriona retrieved the Glock G29 from beneath her pillow. She caught a glimpse of her plaid scarf draped over the chair, and the sight of it tickled something in the back of her brain.

What is it about that scarf—

Oh.

Right.

She wasn't alone in the apartment.

The memory of the kilted drunk slipped into place, completing her puzzle. She'd left him snoring on the dolly in the living room. He must have awoken and, judging by the bouncy noise following the last thud, he was rooting through her kitchen cabinets in search of something to feed his hangover. He wasn't *slamming* the doors, but he wasn't *easing* them either.

She slipped out of bed and crept toward her door. Resting her ear against it, she listened for movement.

Nothing.

Maybe he'd left? She unlocked the door as quietly as she could and cracked it open.

The figure of a muscular man, drawn in early morning shadow, stood six feet from the threshold to her room.

He took a step toward her.

"Hold it right there," she said, revealing her gun.

He stopped parallel with one of the three windows in her apartment. The ambient light glowing from the lot's security lamps revealed her houseguest as naked, his hand covering his naughty bits. Shadows cast by the pronounced ridges of his body stretched across his skin like fingers. If it weren't for the golden hue of his flesh, she would have thought someone had misdelivered a marble statue from one of the ancient Greece sets.

All this guy needs is a fig leaf.

Catriona remained still, dumbfounded by the unusual standoff. The stranger hadn't broken in—she'd *rolled* him in—but she didn't know anything about him, and it was unsettling to have such a large, shaggy, *naked* creature in black boots loose in her living room.

Stranger still, the man's dark, shoulder-length hair blew away from his face as if he were standing atop a Scottish bluff on the cover of a romance novel.

She squinted, confused. Did the musclebound hunk-a-drunk travel with his own breeze? Did he wake up and decide to film a music video in her living room?

A noise somewhere between a hum and roar crept into her consciousness, and she shifted her gaze to the window. The buzz played steadily outside.

"Step back, Kilty," she barked.

He followed her command.

"*More.*"

Catriona moved into the room and leaned forward to peek through her open window.

Outside, men gathered around a giant wind machine, pointed directly into her face. She felt her hair fly backward.

"Hey, Joey, you're blowing me out of my apartment," she called down.

The men looked up. Joey grinned and waved.

"Sorry, Catriona," he called back up, twisting the fan to point away. "Wanted to test it before we took it all the way to sixty-five."

Catriona waved back.

"No prob—*Whoop!*"

An arm hooked her waist, jerking her from the window and lifting her off the ground as if she weighed no more than an oversized teddy bear. Strong fingers clamped around the wrist that held her gun.

"Ye were gonnae shoot an unarmed man?" said a voice in her ear, low and heavy with a Scottish brogue. She could smell the whiskey on his breath.

"Was I going to shoot an unarmed, *naked* man roaming my *home*?" She scoffed, trying to appear less frightened than she was. "Maybe I *was*. I don't think a jury of my peers would—"

"Whit? Whit are ye babbling aboot?"

As he spoke, Catriona stiffened the fingers on her free hand and thrust back, poking the four longest into his throat as she twirled from his grasp. He coughed but still stripped the gun from her grip as she moved.

Counting on being armed at this point, she froze, facing him. He held her pistol in one hand, pointed down at her knees, and his other hand still covered his *built-in* gun with the other.

In the growing sunlight, she saw his body glistening with sweat. She could feel her t-shirt sticking to her back, wet from being pressed against his chest.

"Easy—" She said, holding up her palms.

"Eh?" He looked at the gun and grunted before lowering it as if both tired and disgusted. "Ah wullnae shoot ye."

His pupils took a lap in his skull before returning. He shook his head as if to clear it. She ceased worrying he'd shoot her from malice and grew concerned he'd mistake her for an enemy during a fever dream.

"Why are you so sweaty? Do you have a fever? The flu?" she asked.

"Ah dinna ken."

"*What?*"

"Eh?"

The pistol slid from his hand and clattered to the floor. She balled her arms against her chest, covering, worried the weapon would fire. The Scotsman giggled, his legs wobbling.

"Do you even know where you are?" she asked.

He remained closer to the gun than she did, so she didn't think diving for it was the best call...*yet.* Better to keep him talking.

The Highlander snapped his attention to her as if surprised to find he wasn't alone. He straightened and puffed out his impressive chest. His expression shifted to one of confidence, bordering on bravado, but his eyes telegraphed that a very different song played in his head.

Some kind of wonky circus tune, played at the wrong speed if she had to guess.

She suspected he was moments from passing out. Working for the studio, she'd seen that look *plenty* of times.

Time to take it slow and direct.

"Look, buddy, all I have to do is scream, and you'll never work in this business again. Maybe you think you're being *method*, but how about you put your clothes back on, and *maybe* I'll let you keep your job."

"Is that any way tae treat me after our time t'gither?" he mumbled.

He squeezed his eyes tight, and though she thought it *might* be a good time to run for help, his comment gave her pause.

Our time together?

She scowled. "What are you talking about?"

"Ye kip," he muttered, motioning toward the bedroom.

She scowled. "I found you passed out on the set. *Our time*

together consisted of me hauling you up here like luggage."

He wiped his sweaty brow with the hand not covering his manhood.

"We dinnae share ye kip?" he asked, still pointing at her bedroom.

"My *bed*? Are you asking me if we slept together?"

"Aye. Ah guessed ye a hooer from yer clothes." He waved a hand at the oversized t-shirt that doubled as her nightgown.

Catriona eyes widened. "Did you just call me a *whore*?"

She was about to verbally eviscerate the brute when he blanched, shifting from golden tan to sickly beige in a matter of seconds. Her anger deviated to the type of concern she'd feel for any wounded animal.

"Hey. Take it easy, big guy."

He offered her a lopsided grin, revealing a laugh line deep enough to audition for the role of dimple. He opened his mouth as if to say something before his eyes rolled back into his head, and he collapsed to the ground in a great naked heap.

Scottish Elvis has left the building.

She tilted back her head and sighed, realizing that once again, she would need to move him.

"Why does he keep doing this to me?"

CHAPTER FIVE

"I can see why you called me," said Dr. Noseeum, studying the man curled on Catriona's floor.

The good doctor's real name was Peter Roseum, but everyone at the studio called him "Dr. No-see-um" because he knew how to keep his mouth shut. A discreet doctor was the number-one tool tucked in a studio fixer's belt. From overdoses to botched beauty attempts, Dr. Noseeum had seen it all and repeated *none* of it. He could fix almost anything short of bad facelifts. For bad plastic surgery, Catriona sent Hollywood stars on a private sabbatical far from the prying eyes of the paparazzi until their eyebrows remerged from their hairline like a bunny peeping from the underbrush.

"Just to be clear, this isn't what it looks like," said Catriona.

"No? That's too bad. I thought global warming had finally reached you, ice princess."

She knew she had a reputation for being less than cuddly but didn't appreciate being teased about it. She curled her lip.

"Let it go."

Noseeum chuckled. "So, back to our muscle-bound friend here. Part of me wants to ask why he's curled in the fetal position, but then, I assume *all* the men in your life end up this way."

"That's how he collapsed, smart ass. Just fix him so I can get him out of my apartment."

"Uh-huh. You say you found him drunk?"

"Yes. I mean, I assume so. He smelled like Boston on St. Patrick's day."

Noseeum stood and put his hands on his hips. "Well, the only thing I'm sure of is that this is more than a hangover. He's burning up, and there's a strange wound here over his hip. Looks pretty deep. We need to get him to a hospital."

Catriona groaned. "Can't you work your magic on him? Give him a pill or something?"

"To hazard a guess could cost the man his life. Usually, when you bring me these cases, I at least *know* it's an overdose, or they've been shoving army men into enemy territory—"

Catriona rolled her eyes. "Oh jeez, don't remind me. I still can't figure out how that guy got that plastic tank... *never mind.*" She crossed her arms against her chest and allowed her chin to fall to her chest.

This is what I get for being nice.

She practiced a strict policy of staying as uninvolved with the actors' lives as possible, and now, she'd been forcibly restrained by a naked man who'd had the indecency to collapse on her floor. If an ambulance came to the lot, it would invoke a nightmare of reporters, questions, and—once it was revealed what happened—tittering behind her back for weeks.

"You're *sure* covering him with a blanket and hoping for the best is a *bad* idea?"

Noseeum nodded.

"Fine. I'll take him to the hospital. First, we have to dress him. Roaming the lot with a sweaty, naked man could start rumors."

"You think?"

"Help me move him."

"Help you move him? My whole body weighs the same as his bicep."

She eyeballed the doc. Her friend Dr. Pete was a bird-boned blond standing shy of five-foot-eight inches tall. Adorable like a puppy, but not great for moving furniture or large naked men.

She pointed her index finger at him and swirled it in a

circle. "I've been meaning to talk to you about your whole *body* situation. Could you start working out or something? You'd be a lot handier in these situations if you weren't built like a fifteen-year-old girl."

"Sure. I'll hop right on that."

Catriona closed her eyes and roamed through a mental inventory of the nearest buildings. When she reached Stage Thirty-Two, her lids sprang open.

"Ooh. I know. Go grab me one of those roadie cases. I think there are a bunch of empties on Stage Thirty-two. They're shooting some rocker thing there. I'll dress him, roll him downstairs on the dolly and then we'll pop him in the case and take him to my car."

The doctor frowned. "When exactly did I become your errand boy? I have a medical degree, you know."

She clapped him on the back. "From *Antigua*. When you graduate from Harvard, get back to me. Now go get the case before I take you off the payroll."

With a final disgruntled grumble, Noseeum left to fetch the case.

Catriona took a deep breath.

First things first.

She found what she thought was the man's kilt on the sofa but, in gathering it, found it to be more of a *blanket* than an *article of clothing.*

She looked from the man to the blanket and back again several times, at a loss for how to continue. She found a crude belt, but it didn't seem to be the key to working the ensemble.

"I could have sworn you were wearing this," she said to him. He didn't answer.

What to do? She didn't have anything he could wear...

She grinned as an idea popped into her head.

Catriona stood in the still-closed employment office beneath her apartment with the stranger curled on the dolly. Dr. Noseeum appeared, pushing a large black roadie case.

He grimaced. "What is he wearing?"

"My fuzzy robe."

"It's pink."

"You don't miss a trick."

"Does he not own clothes?"

She frowned. "What he was wearing turned into a blanket overnight. It was either the robe or roll him up like a plaid burrito."

Noseeum stared at her as if poised to say something and then shrugged. He helped her hoist the unconscious man into the case and then rolled it to her Jeep Cherokee. They tilted the box against the opened back of the truck and then slid it inside, accompanied by a symphony of grunting.

"Do you think he can breathe in there?" she asked, gazing at the box.

"Long enough to get him to the hospital and plot his revenge. Do I have to come with you?"

Catriona shut the back of the truck and clapped her hands together. "No. I'm going to dump him out of the case, tell them I found him on the street, and leave him."

"Perfect. If he's dead when you get there, remember: I haven't seen you all day."

"Goes without saying."

He waved. "Ciao."

Noseeum disappeared through the gates, and Catriona hopped into the driver's seat. She pulled the door to shut it, only to have it resist her attempt. It took her a moment to realize a stranger had his hand on the door, holding it open, one hand on the doorframe, the other holding a gun pointed at her face.

The man had a strange lump protruding from the center of his forehead as if he'd tried to grow a unicorn horn and failed.

"Move over," he said, motioning with the barrel of the gun. His accent told her he was a native of the Southeastern United

States.

Catriona closed her eyes, picturing where she'd left her Glock back at the apartment. Her memory was excellent but only worked in pictures. Unfortunately, her particular sort of memory *didn't* work to remind her to grab her gun before wrapping a naked man in a fuzzy robe and rolling him out of her apartment on a dolly. She could picture the gun sitting on her counter and knew the barrel pointed toward the refrigerator—for what *that* was worth.

Unicorn was a stranger. Her quasi-eidetic memory would never have forgotten his burgeoning horn.

"Do I know you?" she asked, looking for a way to stall.

The man shook his head.

"No, and you don't wanna, but it's too late now. *Move over*."

She smiled. "What a lovely accent. Are we shooting a *Deliverance* reboot?"

The man scowled and motioned with the gun. "I said *move it*. Passenger side."

She swung her legs from beneath the steering wheel as if intending to comply but, once clear, dove for the passenger door. Before her fingers touched the handle, it opened, and another man, as gaunt as Unicorn was pudgy, pointed a gun of his own at her head. He was young, but his expression didn't have the *joie de vivre* she might hope for in a boy holding a gun at her face. His stained, cockeyed teeth looked as though he'd been raking the garden with them. The lump in his cheek explained the stains; chewing tobacco. No sooner did she notice it than he spat a brown mass to the ground.

Delightful.

She heard Unicorn's voice behind her. "Get paid the same, missy, dead or alive. You pick it."

Catriona righted herself in the passenger seat. The skinny man hopped into the back seat as Unicorn slid into the driver's spot.

"You can at least tell me what this is about," she said.

The Jeep roared to life. "You'll know soon enough."

CHAPTER SIX

Unicorn pulled into the parking lot of a large storage building, and Skinny exited the Jeep. He opened her door and dragged her from the car by the forearm.

"Easy," she said, jerking from his grasp.

He grunted and pushed her toward the warehouse.

Unicorn joined them, and the two escorted her inside.

The small room they entered was empty but for a wooden chair and a table. On the table sat several zip ties and a black shaving case.

Catriona felt the blood drain from her face. She lifted her chin and forced a chuckle to convince herself all was well.

It was a big, fat *lie*.

She pointed at the chair. "Oh, come *on*. The old interrogation chair trick? I've seen this before. What's next? You tie me over a shark tank?"

Skinny snorted a laugh. "Where we gonna get sharks?" He rolled his eyes as Unicorn, who glared at him with no expression, and then pushed Catriona into the chair.

Catriona tried to bounce to her feet, but Unicorn applied steady pressure to her shoulder, pinching the sinew of her neck as the skinny man pulled back her arms. Her shoulders sang with pain as Skinny secured her wrists with one of the zip ties.

She gritted her teeth.

If this is one of my disgruntled studio assets exacting revenge for making them go to rehab, they've outdone themselves.

She'd never imagined she might *truly* be in danger until the inconvenience of being kidnapped officially turned into false imprisonment. Now, she found it hard to take her eyes off the black leather shaving case on the table. She suspected it did *not* have safety razors and airport-sized shaving cream in it.

Catriona scanned the small room, searching for something to explain her predicament. In her line of work, she had plenty of enemies, but none she'd mentally graduated to *someone who will probably tie me to a chair and torture me* status.

She cleared her throat. "I think this has gone far enough, guys. It's obvious you have the wrong person."

"No, we don't," said Unicorn.

A door leading deeper into the building opened, and a man wearing jeans and a ragged flannel shirt entered. A shockingly red beard hung to the middle of his chest, and he walked with a pronounced limp. Catriona guessed him to be in his early sixties, though it was hard to tell. Everything about him seemed *ragged*.

"Ye work where they make the movies?" he asked.

His accent differed from that of his cohorts, falling somewhere between their southern drawls and the brogue of the man locked in the back of her truck.

Oh no.

In all the kidnapping, she'd forgotten about Naked MacWhiskeybreath. If she was killed, the man in her car might die from his fever or suffocate before anyone found him.

Though, it might serve him right. After all, what were the chances this new guy would have a bit of a Scottish brogue as well? It couldn't be a coincidence...

Were these the people who stabbed Kilty?

She couldn't give him up to the thugs. Her business *was* discretion, and telling the lunatics who captured her about Kilty might put his life in danger as well.

Hopefully, he didn't suffocate.

Note to self: when boxing up feverish men, always add air holes in case I'm kidnapped and murdered during transport.

These were the sorts of things no one ever warned you

about.

Catriona closed her eyes and tried to concentrate.

Stop babbling. Think. Get to the bottom of things.

As soon as the phrase *bottom of things* entered her mind, she had a flash of the Highlander's tush hanging beneath his kilt the night before. She realized the memory must have made her smirk when Redbeard barked at her.

"What's so funny?"

Nerves jangling, she blinked at him, holding his gaze as brazenly as she could muster under the circumstances. Especially since she'd noticed he was wearing black gloves.

Nothing good ever came from hands in black gloves.

"What's this about?" she asked.

The man smiled, but not in any way that put her at ease. He didn't look as if he were recalling a cute wardrobe malfunction the way she'd been. His cheek twitched, and his entire jaw shifted unnaturally to the right.

Catriona swallowed.

What are you?

The man pushed his jaw back into place before speaking. "Ah heard you were seen with a Highlander last night."

Catriona remained expressionless.

The big guy in the trunk *is* the one they want.

She considered her options.

Did she owe Kilty any loyalty? She didn't even know the man.

She opened her mouth to let them know the Highlander was in her Jeep and then feigned a yawn to hide the attempt.

No.

At least don't tell them *yet.*

She needed time to think. They hadn't unpacked the torture instruments yet, and there was one other very good reason to protect Kilty—giving him up would end her usefulness. As long as they thought she had the information they needed, they wouldn't kill her.

Right?

That's how it worked in the movies...

She did her best to look confused. "A *Highlander*? I don't think so. That would be weird."

"Ye didn't find a man in a *feileadh-mór* last night?"

"In a *what*?"

"A great kilt. Didn't ye wheel him to yer home?"

She shook her head. "That would be even weirder."

"Do ye know a man named Ryft?"

"*Ryft*? What kind of name is *Ryft*?"

"Answer the question."

"No. I suppose he's a Highlander, too?"

Redbeard's bushy eyebrows raised. "Aye. So ye do know him?"

"No. But you're obsessed with Highlanders, so I took a stab."

The big man hobbled forward and, without a moment's hesitation, slapped her across the face with his large, open palm. It hurt, but the shock of it numbed her to the actual pain.

True anger swelled in her chest.

Catriona's tongue swabbed the corner of her mouth, the taste of iron feeding her fury.

She set her jaw, her voice low and steady.

"You know the thing about Highlanders?" she asked.

His hand still hung in the air, and his strange jaw clicked. "What?"

She leaned as far forward as her binds would allow as if she was about to share a very important secret.

"There can only be *one*."

The two of them remained, eyes locked until the man released a loud guffaw and put his face in hers. "I saw that movie. I thought there *was* only one until a week ago."

"Wait. Don't tell me. *You*?"

He nodded, his eyes narrowing. "You're a feisty little bitch, aren't ye?"

She remained silent, holding his stare. She'd stopped breathing to avoid his stale breath... and because she was pretty sure she'd forgotten how.

He straightened. "My name is Thorn Campbell. I'm a friend

of Ryft's. We were separated long ago, and I've been looking for him."

She nodded. "Great. Good luck with that. I'd like to leave now."

He crossed his enormous arms over his barrel chest and studied her.

"I think ya know more than yer sayin'."

The skinny man put a hand on her shoulder, and Catriona did the only thing she could do.

She screamed.

Unicorn covered her mouth with his hand, and she bit the fleshy mound of his palm. He yelped and slapped her upward against her nose, causing her eyes to water.

She winced before a thought occurred to her.

He tried to silence me. Does that mean there's someone nearby who can hear?

She screamed again.

CHAPTER SEVEN

It was dark.

Very dark, but for a pinhole of light up and to his left. His knees ached, and he tried to stretch, only to find himself restrained by his surroundings. He reached out and felt the walls. Top, bottom, side to side.

Ah'm in a kist.

Not a proper chest. He could tell how thin the walls were by the sound they made. He took a deep breath and punched straight up.

The top gave way.

Light streamed into his tiny prison. He continued to punch and tear until he'd made a hole big enough to climb through— only to find himself in *another* box. This prison was more spacious but made of stronger stuff. It had windows. He peered outside and saw dirt and a large, square structure that seemed too shiny to be made of wood.

Taking a moment to catch his breath, he attempted to recall the last thing he could remember.

A lassie. A lassie on a bed, asleep.

The memory made him smile. He had no idea who she was or where *he* was, but something about that lassie sleeping made him smile.

No.

Wait.

There was a gun.

Something about that lassie and a gun. She confronted him, stood there in her shift—

A scream split the silence, and he straightened, banging his head on the roof of his new, fancy metal box. It was a woman's scream.

He peered through the window. The scream had to have come from the building.

He tapped on the glass and found it to be thick. Feeling his hip, he realized he no longer wore his kilt but a robe made of strange, soft material, like a rabbit's hide, but in an unnatural color.

A flash of silver running along the edge of the trunk caught his eye, and he tore it away to fold it into a makeshift sword. The metal wasn't sturdy, but it might give an enemy pause, and, in his hands, anything could be a weapon.

Could it? Why do I know that?

No time. He couldn't remember more than the sleeping lassie, but he was *sure* he knew how to fight.

He was about to kick out the window when he noticed an odd latch on the wall. He pushed and pulled at it until he heard a click. Putting his shoulder against the wall, it opened upward until he tumbled out.

He lay on the ground a moment, staring.

His prison was on wheels.

Stranger still.

No time to figure out where he was. A lass had screamed. He had to find out who and why.

Wiping the sweat from his brow on the sleeve of the strange fuzzy robe, he pounded toward the huge square building as a second scream rang out.

CHAPTER EIGHT

The outer door crashed inward, nearly striking Thorn, who stumbled out of the way. Unicorn pulled his gun.

A sweaty man in a pink fuzzy robe filled the entryway, his chest rising and falling with belabored breath. In his hand, he held a long silver square of metal that Catriona guessed had been stripped from the edges of the case in which he'd been locked.

It was good to know the Highlander was alive and breathing. She'd never been happier to see a sweaty giant in a pink fuzzy robe.

The skinny man dove forward. The Highlander flattened him with a single punch to the face. The efficiency of the blow was almost cartoonish, and Catriona barked a laugh without meaning to.

Time to move.

She took the distraction as an opportunity to slide her bound hands up the back of the chair, stand, and kick the gun from Unicorn's hand. He'd been so busy sizing up the intruder that he'd never seen her coming.

His hand free of his gun, Unicorn grabbed her arm and jerked her toward him.

"Take your hands off the lassie," said her new favorite person. More or less. It sounded more like he said *tack yer hauns aff th' lassie,* but it was clear enough what the man she only knew as *Kilty* or *the drunken loser* meant. After all, she was the only *lassie* in the room.

Unicorn looked to his boss.

Redbeard stared at the young man in his doorway.

"It's impossible," he muttered.

Unicorn gave Catriona's arm another jerk. "Thorn. Whatya wanna do?"

Thorn tore his gaze from Kilty.

"Let her go."

The lumpy-headed henchman complied with reluctance. As soon as he freed Catriona's bicep, Kilty reached forward and drew her to *him*. Wherever her skin touched him, her flesh became slick. He felt like a warm, sweaty eel.

Kilty rattled the metal strip toward the two still-standing men and once at the unconscious, skinny man on the floor for good measure.

He backed out of the room, guiding her with him, her arms still tied behind her back. Once outside, he scooped her in his arms and jogged toward the truck.

"They stole yer horses!" he screamed as they neared the vehicle.

"*What?*" She pushed against his chest. "Why are you carrying me? Put me down, idiot. They didn't kneecap me."

"Whit?"

"*Put me down.*"

He stopped and dropped her to her feet. The moment she found her balance, she sprinted for the car, calling to Kilty as she ran.

"I can't drive with my hands tied behind my back. You have to drive."

Catriona glanced back at the building. The two conscious men stood outside now, staring at them, still as statues.

She started around the Jeep and noticed Kilty, pale, standing beside the driver's door.

"Get in."

The wild look in his eyes told her all she needed to know.

"You can't drive, can you?" she asked.

He pursed his lips.

She huffed. "You can't drive. Fine—*whatever*. I've got a knife in the glovebox. Get it and cut me loose. I'll drive."

He continued to stare at her. She looked back at the building and saw her captors still standing, watching.

Why aren't they chasing us?

She was trapped in the middle of the most ineffectual, longest escape *ever*. How long could their luck hold out?

"Hurry." She hissed at her baffled savior, nodding hard to the right. "The other side of the truck. *Open the door.* There's a box in front of the seat. Open it and *get me the knife*."

Kilty jumped into action as if he'd been shocked-to with defibrillator paddles. Sprinting around the truck, he fumbled with the door before finally throwing it open and retrieving the pocket knife. He held it out toward her.

"What am I going to do with that? *Cut me free,* you oaf."

"Och." He nodded and cut the zip tie from her hands, muttering beneath his breath as he worked the blade through the tough plastic.

Catriona kept her eyes locked on her captors, but still, they seemed content to watch her and Kilty fumble through their grand escape. The skinny man joined them, a sheet of blood pouring from his nose.

He, too, stared.

She circled back and hopped into the driver's seat. She'd watched Unicorn toss the keys on the floor when they'd arrived.

Please let them still be there. Please let them still be there...

They were.

Starting the vehicle, she waited a moment for Kilty to enter the passenger side. Instead, she felt the truck shake.

He'd jumped in the back.

She looked over her shoulder and found him squatting, the hatch still wide open.

"What are you—*never mind*. Let's get the hell out of here."

She tore down the dirt road leading away from the building.

Something inside of Catriona worried it was all a trap. The

strange way her captors watched their escape—the only explanation was that the truck would explode before they drove ten feet, or a blockade would keep them from getting far—

Nothing happened.

When they hit the highway, she remembered again to breathe.

Kilty spoke. She jumped. She'd almost forgotten about the sweaty titan crouching in her cargo area.

"Ah wid hay come sooner, but they locked me in a chest."

They. Catriona realized Kilty thought the *bad guys* locked him in the roadie case.

No reason to correct him.

"No problem."

"Howfur dae ye go sae fast withoot horses?" he asked, glimpsing over his shoulder at the retreating road behind him.

She scowled. "*What?* Hey, who *are* you, anyway? What's your name?"

The man clung to the backseat headrest, one hand on his temple as if his head hurt.

"Hello? What's your *name*?" she repeated.

He gasped and looked up, wide-eyed.

"*Brochan.* Ah mind it noo. It's *Brochan.*"

She glanced at the rearview.

"Did you say your name is *broken*?"

"Aye. Brochan. Broch. Those men. Whit did they want wi' ye?"

"I think they might be after *you*, though they didn't chase you." She shook her head, still baffled. "The way he *stared* at you like he saw a ghost. Do you know the guy with the red beard?"

"Na. Was one of them yer husband?"

She laughed. "My *husband*? No. Is that how men treat their wives where you come from?"

"Are ye married?"

"No, and what the hell does that have to do with anything?"

He peered between the back headrests at her until she became unnerved.

"Why are you staring at me?"

"A'm trying tae figure whit's wrong with ye."

"*Nothing's* wrong with me."

Catriona pulled to the side of the road and slammed the Jeep into park. She twisted to glare at him.

"Is there somewhere I can take you? I think getting far away from you might be good for my health."

He shrugged. "Aye. Ye can take me to Glenorchy."

"Glenorchy." She sighed. "Is that in Scotland by any chance?"

"Aye."

"We're still doing this then? You're still pretending you're a Highlander?"

He puffed out his chest, and the fuzzy pink robe separated, revealing the curve of his impressive pectorals. He set his jaw and stared daggers at her.

"Ah *am* a Hielanman."

She jerked her gaze from his body to his face. It only seemed right, what with him looking so *serious* all of a sudden.

"You know I have no influence on casting decisions, right?" she asked.

He waved a hand at her. "Ah dinnae understand ye, wummin, but ye hae control o'er the bewitched carriage, sae take me where ye wish, and ah will fin mah own way home."

She laughed. "*Bewitched carriage.* That's funny. I wish it *was* bewitched. It would be cheaper to fill the tank with witches."

She put the car back into drive but kept her foot on the brake as she spoke. "You're right. I do have control over the *bewitched carriage*. I'm going to take you to Sean's. Maybe he can talk some sense into you. He might at least be able to understand you."

He shrugged and made a scoffing noise.

"Pull that door shut," she added.

"Eh?"

"The back hatch. *Pull it shut.* We can't keep driving with it open."

He leaned forward and lowered the hatch, which made him look even more oversized, hunched in her SUV amongst the torn remnants of the roadie case.

CHAPTER NINE

"Shouldn't we git 'em?" said the skinny man standing beside Thorn Campbell. His nose slanted at an unnatural angle, and his lip and teeth glistened red with blood.

Thorn held up a hand. "Nah. Hold."

The man with the lump on his head peered around Thorn. "You look like ground meat, Jesse."

The skinny man snarled. "Shut up, Knotty. At least *my* face will heal in a couple of days."

They watched the man in the fuzzy pink robe jump into the back of the SUV. A moment later, the woman, already in the driver's seat, peeled the Jeep out of the parking lot.

"Was that the guy? Was that Ryft?" asked Jesse.

"Nah, you eejit. Ye think I would have let him go?" Thorn reached out and clamped his fingers on either side of the skinny man's crooked nose before snapping it back into place.

Jesse screamed and cursed, stumbling away, his hands covering his face.

Thorn grunted. "You'll thank me later, boy."

Jesse glared at him from behind his fingers.

"She'll be easy enough to find again," said Knotty. His real name was John, but he'd been nicknamed for the permanent lump in the center of his head that made him look like a knotty pine tree. As a child, his brother had been chopping wood when the head of the ax came loose. Had the sharpened end led,

Knotty would be dead, but as it was, he caught the back end, suffering nothing more than a concussion and a peculiar, permanent lump.

He never stood behind people swinging axes again.

Jesse returned to the group, his eyes watering and expression pinched in pain. "I guess if he's one of those Scottish dudes, he's as comfortable in a fuzzy robe as he is in one of them skirts."

Thorn's palm flashed, smacking Jesse in the nose again, and he spun away, wailing.

"It's not a *skirt*. It's a *kilt*."

"So, we're looking for a *different* Scottish guy?" asked Knotty.

Thorn nodded. "He's old now. I showed ye the shot from the TV. Did you see him in a kilt then?"

"No, Boss. But—"

Thorn stepped forward, and Knotty winced as if expecting a slap of his own.

"But *what*?" asked Thorn.

"It's just weird, don't ya think? That we're looking for a guy ya say came from Scotland when you did, and we *found* a Scottish guy, but not the right one?"

Thorn's rage dissipated, and he limped away, stabbing his cane hard into the dirt with each step.

"It's stranger than ye think."

Thorn thought it had been pure chance he'd spotted Ryft in the background of an entertainment news report. Forty years had aged the man, but there was no mistaking him. He had the same look—that expression that said he knew he was better than everyone else.

Thorn couldn't get from Tennessee to Hollywood fast enough.

His men watched the Parasol Pictures lot for a week and a half before they spotted the girl, dragging a Highlander on a wheeled cart from one building to another.

It couldn't be a coincidence.

Maybe he shouldn't have let them go, but the sight of that

boy—

"Why didn't I look for him?" he screamed suddenly, holding his arms out in front of him as if begging the universe to answer.

"For who, boss?" asked Knotty.

"*Ryft*. When I first came, when I was in the diner—he *had* to be nearby." He hobbled back to the men. "Those two know Ryft, I'd wager on it. The girl—"

"The girl said she didn't," said Knotty.

Jesse took a step back but remained more than arm's length from Thorn. "Yeah, Boss, she looked clueless. Too bad she got away." He leered at Knotty. "I was lookin' forward to gettin' the info out of her."

Thorn shot them both a look, and they sobered.

"You want us to go after 'em? We could still maybe catch 'em?" suggested Knotty.

Thorn shook his head. "No. Ryft's going to come to *us*. We missed our chance to get the drop on him, but he'll come if he knows I'm here. I know the man. We'll make it easy for him to find us and be ready when he shows up."

Jesse nodded. "That's why you're the boss."

Thorn glanced at him. "I'm the boss because you two are dumb as posts."

CHAPTER TEN

They drove in silence for several miles while Catriona rolled the events of the morning around in her mind. She didn't know what those men wanted, but she *was* glad Brochan showed up. He'd been a tad less terrifying in a fuzzy robe, but in the right costume, he would have looked like Superman.

He'd saved her life, after all.

What was strange was that it all felt *familiar*. When the stranger appeared with his makeshift sword, Catriona caught a glimpse of a memory. A man holding her as a child—a sword in his hand. A terrible man she'd known as a guardian lay dead on the ground, cleft from shoulder to chest.

In her mind's eye, she looked up at the man holding her.

He looked like the Highlander.

No. *Stupid.* It was *Sean*, of course, who had saved her from the terrible man when she was young.

Why would she see the stranger's face?

She'd been so young—

With her mind drifting, the truck began to as well. She jerked the wheel to straighten and heard the man in the back grunt with displeasure.

She glanced in the rearview. "Sorry. And, thank you, by the way. You saved me from who knows what, and I *do* appreciate it."

He shrugged and removed the pink robe. She heard him

thrashing. His naked knees and black-booted feet appeared above the back seats like antennae. A flash of red and green tartan caught her eye, and she realized he was attempting to re-wrap his kilt. She wished she had a better view because how that blanket turned into an article of clothing, she had *no* idea.

His head popped up.

"Where's mah *lèine cròiche*?"

"Your what?"

"Mah *shirt*."

"Oh. It's not there?"

"No."

"Oh. Hm. Sorry. I must have—I mean—those men must have lost it."

He grunted and turned away from her. She could see the muscles in his back flexing as he resumed dressing. Distracted by the undulating sinews, she had to yank the wheel a second time as she caught the edge of the road.

His shoulder punched against the side of the cabin as the Jeep jumped to the left.

She held up a hand. "Sorry."

"Ye drive this carriage like a demon," he muttered.

"You could have sat in a *seat* like a human being," she retorted.

Over an hour later, they reached Sean's high desert home in Lucerne Valley. Though he had an apartment in the city, he preferred to be far away from Hollywood whenever possible. He'd turned most of the more *covert* studio operations over to her and the day-to-day security to his second in command, Big Luther. Sean retired to his ranch house, nestled in the middle of nowhere, every chance he got.

Catriona pulled into the long winding drive and parked. Hopping out, she walked to the back of the vehicle and opened it.

Broch squinted into the sun and pushed past the torn chunks of the case to exit. He stood before her bare-chested, his kilt once again around his waist, the top half hanging in a bunch behind him. She eyed the wound above his hip, two inches wide, red and angry. Dried blood stains flecked the fuzzy robe laying in a heap inside the Jeep.

"That wound is nastier than I remember," she said, raising a hand toward it.

He flinched from her touch. "Tis a scratch."

"Tis *infected*. You have a fever. You passed out."

He arched an eyebrow. "When did *ye* see this wound?"

Catriona hemmed.

Shoot. He was about to piece together that *she* was responsible for putting him in a roadie case, not the kidnappers.

He offered her a disapproving scowl. She ignored him until his gaze shifted to scan the vast empty desert surrounding Sean's home.

"Whit is this place? Is it hell?"

She chuckled. "Depends on who you ask. Come inside."

Catriona walked to the door of the adobe rancher and knocked before entering. Sean never locked his door. Unless the coyotes grew fingers, there wasn't much point.

She held the door open for Broch, and he entered, eyes darting left and right as if he expected an enemy to leap from every corner. She realized he'd somehow shortened and sharpened the metal stripping from the case and now held it in his hand like a knife.

She pointed to the makeshift blade. "We're safe here. Give that to me."

He glanced at her hand before sliding the metal across his taut stomach, tucking the blade into the top of his kilt. His gaze never left hers, as if he were daring her to ask for his weapon a second time.

She shrugged. "Fine. Sean can take care of himself. Even against a big, strapping weirdo."

Walking into the living room, she called for Sean.

"Out by the pool," returned a man's voice.

Catriona led her wary visitor through the house and opened folding doors leading to a paved patio with a small turquoise pool in the center. Sean sat in a comfortable outdoor chair wearing swimming trunks, a book sitting open on his lap.

He was in his mid-sixties, with short salt-and-pepper hair and a tightly trimmed beard. Longer hair in the same hues grew wild on his chest. Wrinkles spidered on either side of his tawny eyes as he grinned upon seeing her.

"Hey, sweetheart."

As his gaze shifted to Broch, his eyebrows rose on his forehead like furry caterpillars scaling a wall.

His mouth fell open, but no sound escaped.

"Sean?" said Catriona, hoping to prod him back to the present.

He shook his head. "Sorry. So, now we trot in with half-naked men?" He stood and extended his hand in greeting. "*Sean. You are?*"

The Highlander offered a sharp nod. "Brochan."

The men shook hands. It looked to Catriona as if Sean couldn't tear his gaze off the young man.

"He's background talent, in case you're wondering about the outfit," she said.

Sean's bushy brows knit. "We aren't filming any Highland pictures now." He gestured to Broch's waist. "Do you always enter a man's home with a *knife* in your belt?"

"Ah'd prefer tae keep it if ye dinnae mind. We've had trouble."

"Trouble?" Sean's attention shot to Catriona.

She pulled a chair to sit and relayed the story of finding Broch, the kidnapping, Redbeard, Unicorn, and the rest, careful to leave out the part where she and Noseeum stuffed the Highlander in a box.

The frown never left Sean's face. "Did you get a name? What did they want?"

She jerked a thumb toward Broch. "That's what I need to get out of *him*."

Broch put his hand on his chest. "Me?"

Catriona had decided to wait until she was safe beside Sean before questioning Broch about his involvement with her kidnappers. She'd seen enough movies to know smart people never confronted others with accusations while *alone* with them.

It never ended well.

She nodded to the Highlander. "I saw the way Thorn Campbell's face changed when he saw you, and he had a bit of your accent—"

Sean cut her short. "Who?"

"*Thorn Campbell.* That was the guy's name. Redbeard."

Sean blanched and Catriona put her hand on his. "Are you okay?"

He nodded. "What did he look like, this Thorn Campbell?"

"Big, barrel-chested man, your age, big red beard. Like some kind of leprechaun Santa Claus."

Sean fell quiet and stared at the pavers.

"Should I take it from your reaction that *you* know this guy? Does this have something to do with the studio, after all? Or do all Scots know each other?"

Sean's hard expression softened. "No, no. The name's familiar, but I'm having trouble placing it."

"Maybe this will help. Do you know anyone named Ryft?"

Sean adopted a blank expression, but not before his eyes flashed with recognition. Catriona felt a wave of anxiety.

He's hiding something from me.

Sean shook his head and turned to Broch. "*Có ás a tha thu?*"

"Glenorchy. Thu?"

"*Glenorchy cuideachd.*"

Catriona put her flat palms on the table. "Whoa. Why are you two talking like aliens?"

The corner of Sean's mouth curled. "Do you think this man is so dedicated to his craft that he learned Scottish Gaelic to be background talent?"

"That's what you're speaking?"

Sean nodded.

"So, he *is* from the Highlands?"

"It would appear so."

"But how did he get on my lot?"

"That's a question to ask Big Luther. Seems security has lapsed. I might have to go in and kick some butt."

"Stop bletherin' aboot me lik' ah'm nae sitting here," said Broch, glaring back and forth between Catriona and Sean.

Sean chuckled. "I apologize."

Catriona sized up her kilted problem. "I can't fly him to Scotland. What am I supposed to do with him?"

"And there ye gae again. Lik' ah'm nae here."

Broch winced, and Catriona noticed he'd begun to sweat again.

"He has a wound on his side. I think it's infected," she said.

Sean stood. "Let's see it."

With some hesitation, Broch stood and pulled down the side of his kilt, revealing more of both the wound and the lower abdomen muscle running from his hip to parts unknown beneath the kilt. Catriona recalled once seeing two famous actors high-five each other in celebration of developing that lower ab *V* for their movie roles.

Ridiculous.

Those actors did almost nothing but work out. How *boring.* Kilty might be fooling Sean with his Scottish language skills, but everything about him said *actor scamming for a leg up.*

Maybe he'd even staged the kidnapping somehow, *just to save her.*

Hm.

"What happened?" asked Sean, motioning to the wound.

The Highlander shrugged. "Ah dinnae ken."

The older man stood and put his hand on Broch's arm. "*Dé am miastadh a tha thusa ris*?"

Broch put his hand over his heart. "*Chan eil a bheag. Adbuir.*"

Catriona sighed. "You two need to cut that out."

Sean nodded. "Catriona, take him to the spare room and clean and dress that wound. You know where the antibiotics are."

She scowled. "You're *awfully* okay with all of this nonsense. Are you going to adopt him like a puppy because he speaks your alien language? You don't think he's up to something?"

She glared at Broch, daring him to deny the charge.

The Highlander smiled. "Ah saved yer life, lassie. If ah wanted tae hurt ye, ah wid hae left ye there."

Sean smiled. "He's got a point."

Catriona huffed.

"Fine. Let's go. Follow me, *Kilty*."

She led Broch to the spare room and pointed to the bed.

"Sit."

Catriona gathered supplies from Sean's emergency closet and then returned to the spare room. She'd spent most of her young life cleaning the various cuts, stabs, and occasional bullets Sean caught in the line of duty, so she knew where the supplies were kept.

Anyone who thought Hollywood was glamorous needed to spend a week at Sean's house.

She found her patient sitting on the edge of the bed when she returned. She eyed his kilt.

Do we go up or down?

"Stand up and—"

He stood and reached to lift his skirt.

"Nope. *Down*. Pull the edge of your skirt *down*."

His lips drew into a tight line.

"Tis nae a *skirt*. Ye cannae keep callin' me *Kilty* and then call mah kilt a *skirt*, kin ye?" Hooking his thumb at the top of the kilt, he pulled it below the cut.

She knelt beside him and, with a warm wet cloth, did her best to clean the wound. He winced, the muscle on the side of his jaw flexing as he grit his teeth.

"This is deeper than I thought. Do you remember being stabbed?"

"Na."

"What's the last thing you remember?"

He looked at her. "Afore I broke oot of the box? Keekin at ye."

"Keekin? What's *keekin*?"

"Ah saw ye. Thro' the glass." He pointed above Sean's door.

"Through the—" She realized what he was saying and felt her face grow warm. "You looked through the transom window above my bedroom door?"

"Aye. Ye was in yer kip."

"Why were you spying on me?"

He scowled. "Ah dinnae ken ye were in there, did ah?"

She poked him lightly with the tip of the swab she'd been using to apply the antibiotic, and he flinched.

"Don't spy on me again," she grumbled.

"Ah wullnae."

"You better not. And it's *know,* not *ken*. You didn't *know* I was there. If you're going to speak English, speak *English*."

He scoffed. "Yer a hard one."

She stuck a large adhesive bandage to the wound and rubbed down the edges, her fingers brushing that V ridge.

She had to admit, the feel of it beneath her fingertips wasn't unpleasant.

She noticed a tiny smirk on his lips.

"What's so funny?"

His smile grew, and he ran his hand through his shaggy locks. "Ah wis thinking ye dinnae need worry ah'd keek at ye again."

"*Peek*. Not *keek*. But no, I would hope not. You said you wouldn't."

His grin grew broader. "Aye. Ah dinnae need tae. Ah've already seen ye." He tapped his skull with his index finger. "And yer up here noo."

CHAPTER ELEVEN

He watched the women encircle his bed, staring down at him with such love he could feel their gazes warm his flesh.

"Och, he's aff tae be a handsome lad."

"Like his father."

The women tittered with nervous laughter.

Broch sat up, panting.

The women.

He remembered.

My mothers.

He scanned the room but found no way to reconcile the memory of his mothers with the place he'd awoken.

Standing, he stretched and felt the bandage on his hip pull against his tender flesh. He touched it and remembered Catriona.

A very different sort of woman.

She didn't wear a dress, much like his mother Blair. He could picture Blair teaching him to wield a sword. She was taller than him when he was a teen and braver than most men he knew.

Blair preferred the company of women. Perhaps Catriona did as well? He hadn't considered the possibility.

On the other hand, Catriona had things in common with his other mothers as well. She practiced healing arts like his mother Rose. Rose, the side of her face and body riddled with twisting scars from where they'd tried to burn her for witchcraft. Rose told him how the skies had opened and rained salvation upon her, extinguishing the flames. Mother Blair found her and carried her body away to heal, staving off those who yearned to relight the fire once the storm had passed.

Watching over them all was Mother Margaret, once a nun, now the keeper of an inn for abandoned and abused women. The villagers called them *the Broken Women.*

My mothers. Margaret told him they'd found him as a baby, left on their doorstep. Yes, he remembered bits and pieces of his childhood now, but little else.

It was infuriating.

Broch padded barefoot down the hallway of Sean's home, passing a closed but unsealed door. He peered inside and spotted Catriona asleep in the clothes she'd been wearing. Her hand curled and tucked against her lips like that of a sleeping child.

No keekin'. She'd warned him.

He continued down the hall, certain she hadn't seen him. He hoped not. The mouth on that girl could frighten a banshee, but there *was* a softness to her, too. She hid it well, but he sensed it.

Sliding open the large doors, he walked into the night, where a pool of bright blue water glowed as if by magic. He spotted the light source embedded in the wall at one end. Opposite the light, stairs led into the depths. He touched the water with his toe and found it warm. Much warmer than the waters of Glenorchy.

Broch moved to the stairs and entered one step at a time, wary the glowing water might be enchanted. In to the bottom of his kilt and suffering no ill effect, he stepped out, disrobed, and returned to bathe.

"We have a shower," said a voice.

Hip deep and a second from diving headfirst, Broch searched for the source of the voice. The old man, Sean, sat at the same table where he'd met him earlier.

"Ah dinnae see ye."

Sean stood and walked from the shadows.

"What's the last thing you remember, Broch?"

"Entering this glowing loch."

"No, I mean before you rescued Catriona from those men."

Broch tried hard to find a memory other than peering down on Catriona in her bed. He didn't think Sean would appreciate that story.

"Ah was at her home. There was a great metal chest with food inside."

"The refrigerator?"

He shrugged.

"You don't remember anything before that? Anything about where you were raised? You said you knew you were from Glenorchy."

"Aye. Ah mind that. And just noo ah remembered mah mothers."

Sean's expression lit. "Isobel?"

Broch scowled. "No. Blair, Rose, and Margaret. The villagers called them *the Broken Women*. They took me in as a laddie." He cocked his head. "Who's Isobel?"

Sean ignored his question. "Your name, Brochan. Did these women name you?"

"They…" Broch looked away, recalling a conversation. He opened his hand and studied his palm. "They named me after mah hand. Rose tellt me mah timeline was broken."

"Could one of the women have been your birth mother?"

"Na. Of that, ah'm sure."

"So they took you in like I did Catriona?"

"Yer nae her father?"

"No. I found her—in a bad way—during one of my jobs. She'd been orphaned, so I brought her home. I taught her my business because it's the only thing I had to share."

"Whit's yer business?"

Sean sighed. "At my best, I protect people. Fix wrongs. I do what I can to help people find their path."

"And at yer worst?"

"I bend the rules to offer people a second chance."

"That doesn't sound so ill."

"There are worst ways to spend a life or two." Sean crossed his arms against his chest. "Would you like a job, Broch?"

"Workin' for ye?"

"Yes. Me and Catriona. Could you work for a woman?"

Broch chuckled. "If whit ah'm remembering is right, I've always worked for women. Whit do ye want me tae do?"

"I'd like you to do what Catriona asks you to do, but most of all, protect *her*."

"From who?"

"Everyone and everything. But most of all, that red-bearded bastard you saw earlier."

Broch scowled. "Ah kin dae that."

"Deal." Sean smiled and leaned down to shake Broch's hand. "Can you read?"

"Aye. Mother Margaret taught me. Kin speak and read a wee bit of French and Spanish—though at the moment ah dinnae ken how come. The French might have been Rose."

"Great. When you're done swimming, I'll find you some clothes so you don't stick out quite as much. Though with the size of you, it might not matter."

Sean grabbed a towel from a trunk and dropped it beside the pool before returning to his chair.

Broch bathed and stepped out. As he reached to grab the towel, he caught a flash of movement in the window but saw nothing when he looked directly.

He wrapped the towel around himself, a question weighing heavily on his mind.

"Sean, can ah ask you something?"

"Of course."

"The memories ah'm having of the women wha raised me. The more details ah mind, the more it seems to me that ah'm farther from home than ah think. Mah question is: whit *year* is it?"

Sean grimaced and chewed the inside of his cheek for a moment. "Let me ask you this. What year do you think it *should* be?"

"Seventeen forty-nine."

Sean chuckled. "You're wrong by nearly three hundred years."

Broch nodded. "Ah wis feart o' that."

"Sit a moment." Sean nodded toward the chair opposite his own. "I think we need to talk."

CHAPTER TWELVE

Catriona watched Sean and Broch chatting beside the pool.

What could they be discussing at five-thirty in the morning?

Sean disappeared, and Broch swam from the shallow end to the deep and back again with deliberate, powerful strokes. He stood in the shallow end, splashing as if bathing until Sean returned with a towel. Soon after, Broch climbed the stairs, the dimple on the side of his naked posterior flexing with each step.

She looked away. How many times could she see the stranger naked in a week? Too many times, and it would cease to feel like an accident.

Keeping her eyes averted for what she thought was an appropriate amount of time, she returned her attention to the pool. The light from the water danced across the topography of Broch's back as he wrapped the towel around his trim waist.

He has to be a jerk. No one who looked like that was ever *nice*. The vanity it took to keep a body in that kind of shape precluded the possibility of him having any depth. She knew. Working for the studio, she'd been propositioned by more actors, body doubles, and stuntmen than she cared to remember. She'd grown up with terrible men. As a child, she'd run away from terrible men. Now she spent all her time fixing the problems of terrible men.

But that didn't mean she had to *date* terrible men.

Fool me once, shame on you…

Refusing to date men who were vain, dim, vapid, wannabe actors or musicians—in Los Angeles—left few options remaining. Her last date had been with an accountant from payroll. He'd been nice enough, but to say their relationship lacked fire would be an understatement. Her job didn't bring her in contact with many *normal* guys—

Catriona gasped and dropped to the floor.

She'd been so busy recalling her dating woes she hadn't noticed Broch's head swiveling in her direction.

Crap. Now he's going to think I was staring at him.

No doubt he was used to being ogled and probably thought she was yet another woman rendered weak in the knees by his perfect abs.

Ugh. The thought made her furious. She vowed to never look at him again. Why was he even still here? Granted, she owed him a little gratitude for saving her life, but enough was enough.

She crawled beneath the window and placed herself at the kitchen table, where she could pretend she'd been for some time. She heard someone enter the living room and grabbed a magazine. A few minutes later, Sean appeared.

"Coffee?" he asked.

"Sure." She stared at his back as he made coffee, waiting for him to reveal his clandestine *tête-à-tête* with the strapping Scotsman. He turned on the coffee machine, pulled out a chair, and sat at the table, only to tuck his nose into a magazine of his own.

Silence.

She dropped her reading material. "Fine. I'll bite. What were you two talking about?"

"Who?"

"You and the lizards. Who do you think I mean?"

"The boy?" Sean shrugged, his nose never leaving the magazine. "Nothing."

Catriona smoldered. "Dammit, Sean. Who is this guy? Do you know him?"

He looked at her, expressionless. "You're the one who

brought him here."

"I *know*. I didn't know what else to do with him, and I had to tell you about my day with Redbeard. But now, you're out there like you're his pool boy, handing him towels—do you know him? Is he an actor?"

"I don't think so. He could be, though, huh? Handsome lad—"

"Yeah, yeah. Did he tell you anything?"

"Like what?"

"Like why I found him passed out on the lot? Like who stabbed him? Like how he learned to fight like he did?"

"You were impressed?"

"He hit a guy so hard, the dude snapped straight like a piece of lumber and clattered to the ground. It was *ridiculous*."

Sean clucked his tongue. "Sounds like a handy guy to have around."

Catriona shook her head. "Oh *no*. You're not thinking of *hiring* him, are you?"

"What if I was?"

"We don't even know who he *is*. Are we going to overlook the fact that his only possession is a plaid blanket he *wears*?"

"It's a *Breacan an Fhéilidh*."

"A what? You sound like you're coughing up a hairball."

"A *Breacan an Fhéilidh*. A belted plaid."

"Whatever. It's weird. Does he even have a home? Or are you just going to address his paychecks to Scotland?"

Sean chuckled. "Look. I've talked to him—"

"I know. In a language I can't understand. You can cut that out, too."

"Sorry. I asked him where he was from in Scotland and if his intentions were good."

She scoffed. "Let me guess—he said his intentions were all roses and candy. Great. Now we're in the clear."

"He's new to town, and he needs a break. Set him up in that spare apartment above payroll."

Catriona gaped. "He's going to live on the lot? Next door to *me*?"

"Makes sense, doesn't it?"

"Big Luther is going to lose his *mind*."

"He won't be working with Big Luther. He'll be working with you. You're going to teach him your end of the business."

"*I'm* going to teach him—" Catriona put her face in her hands and took a deep breath. "Fine. Let's forget about Kilty for a second. What about Thorn Redbeard and his pet Unicorn?"

"I'm going to look into them today. You worry about Broch."

"*Thorn kidnapped me.* I think I have the right to be involved."

"I'll take care of it."

"You know him, don't you?"

Sean's brow knit. "Broch? No. I told you—"

"Not Broch. *Thorn.*"

He held her gaze. "No."

She frowned.

He looked me in the eye and lied to me.

She sighed. "Hey. On another note, did you kill a man with a sword when you found me? Cut his arm clean off at the shoulder?"

Sean paled. "*What?*"

"I had this memory of a man—"

He cut her short and raised his paper. "You're crazy."

"But—"

Broch entered the room wearing jeans and a t-shirt.

"Good mornin'," he said, arching his back and twisting his hip. He grimaced, and Catriona could see the jeans were a touch too small for him. The jeans had it easy. She could almost *hear* his t-shirt screaming for mercy as it strained across his pecs.

"Those are your clothes? He looks like he's wearing a denim condom."

Sean chuckled. "They'll work until you can get him his own."

Catriona straightened. "Until *I* can? You hire a guy with no apartment, no vehicle, or *clothes,* and now I'm his personal shopper? Is he even legal? Does his kilt have a secret pocket where he keeps his work visa? Does he have a last name?"

Broch grimaced and looked away.

She glared at Sean.

"He *doesn't* have a last name?"

Sean shrugged. "It's his memory—"

She rolled her eyes. "Even people in witness protection and *criminals on the lam* have last names. How can he not have a last name?" Catriona's phone buzzed, and she fished it from her pocket to look at the text.

She groaned.

"For the love of—it's Jaxon's assistant. He's got an emergency. Naturally."

"Take the boy," said Sean.

Catriona stood. "You mean Kilty MacNameless? Sure. Why not? Come on, stranger, you're coming with me. If you can walk in those pants."

"Ah kin walk," muttered Broch. He cocked his head. "We wilnae be riding, though, will we?"

Catriona snatched her keys from the table. "No. We won't be *riding*. My horse is in the shop."

She offered Sean one last glare.

It had no effect.

Sean's expression danced with nothing but amusement as she led Broch from the house.

CHAPTER THIRTEEN

"Take it easy, Jaxon."

Broken glass lay at Catriona's feet. Above her, teen star Jaxon Pike stood on a balcony devoid of any safety barrier. He'd kicked away the glass and framework and stood on the edge, two stories above a cement pool surround. His fingers coiled around the twig-like bicep of a sobbing young woman. Jaxon roared a rambling lyric, from which it was possible to infer that the girl's cheating had both broken his heart and caused a hole in the ozone layer.

He jerked her closer to the edge.

Jaxon's manager, Chad, who stood a safe distance from the drop zone, mumbled, "That's not half bad."

Catriona glanced at him. "What's not *bad* about your client threatening to kill a girl?"

He shook his head. "Oh, *that's* bad. I meant the line about her putting a hole in the ozone of his heart. That could be a hit."

Catriona rubbed her eyes. "That's what I love about you, Chad. You're a real silver-lining kind of guy."

Broch stood behind her, staring up at the struggling couple, one flattened palm shielding his eyes from the sun. "Ye should dae something aboot that."

Catriona nodded. "Great idea, Kilty. Thanks for the input. What did I do before you showed up?"

Chad stepped closer and spoke in Catriona's ear. "What's

with the hunk? Is he one of those Thunder from Down Under strippers?"

"That's a Scottish accent, idiot. Not Australian."

Chad seemed to mull this new information. "He need a manager? Can he sing?"

She glared at him, and he stepped back into the safety zone.

I need to think.

Jaxon Pike had starred in the studio's latest high-octane thriller for youth, *Teen Cop*. He was a double threat; actor/singer as well as drinker/drug abuser. He'd been trouble during the filming of the first movie, but—to Catriona's chagrin—the picture did well despite his dubious acting skills. They'd kept him on to do the sequel.

"Is he aff tae hurt her?" asked Broch.

"Depends what he's on." She glanced at Chad. "What's he on?"

His gaze darted in her direction. "Jax? He's clean, Cat. He's been clean—"

She held up a palm. "Save it. Let me know now, and maybe you won't spend the next fifty years earning twenty percent of his prison allowance."

He sighed. "Meth. Maybe X. Mostly meth. Probably."

She looked at Broch.

"Yes. He's *aff tae hurt her*."

Catriona noted the witnesses: a boy Jaxon's age holding up his camera phone and two teary-eyed young women clinging to each other as they screamed supportive phrases like *Hold on, Brynlee!* at regular intervals.

Catriona watched Broch wander away from the drama toward the sideyard, his eyes downcast.

I guess the big guy doesn't have the stomach for this sort of thing.

Jax was hugging the girl now, rocking back and forth, mumbling. The girl looked like a spooked horse, eyes wild and ringed with white. Both Catriona and Brynlee knew the next outburst would probably be the one that sent her over the edge.

Catriona side-eyed Chad. "Quick question. What was the

last thing I said to you a few months ago when we were in a similar situation?"

"You said to keep him away from drugs. But—"

"And what is he *on*, Chad?"

"*Drugs.* I'm so sorry. *Please.* You have to help him. You always know what to do. He's had a really bad week. He was supposed to get the *Rolling Stone* cover, and they bumped him."

Broch sauntered back into view, rolling something in his hand. Catriona didn't have time to walk him through how to handle situations like this. She had to talk Jaxon down from his perch, get the girl somewhere safe, clear the crowd, and keep the story from spreading—

Broch cocked his arm and threw something in Jaxon's direction. Catriona followed the object's path in time to see it strike the boy between the eyes.

What the—

Jaxon's hands unwrapped from the girl and jerked to either side as he fell backward, out of view.

He'd been holding Brynlee suspended, and, released from his counterweight, she spilled over the edge. Catriona lunged to break the girl's fall, only to smack into Broch's back. She bounced off of him as the girl fell safely into his arms.

Catriona sat on the ground, watching as the Highlander lowered the shaking girl to the pavement.

"Ye'r safe noo, lassie." Broch ran his hand once along the curve of Brynlee's skull, like a father soothing a frantic child. The girl stared into his eyes as if hypnotized. Her shaking ceased.

 The two girls who'd been watching the drama ran to their friend, breaking her trance with their collective hysterics. Brynlee collapsed, sobbing, into their arms, and they pulled her toward the nearest lounge chair.

Catriona realized she, too, had been mesmerized by the scene until she heard a celebratory *whoop!* behind her. The other teenage boy had caught the whole ordeal on his phone and couldn't contain his excitement.

She pointed to him. "*Broch.* That guy. Grab his phone—

Quick! Before he can upload anything." She prayed he hadn't had the forethought to live stream.

Broch's brow knit. "Eh?"

"The thing in his *hand*, bring it to me."

The young man realized he'd been seen and locked eyes with Broch. Terrified, he turned to run, but even in his restrictive borrowed jeans, the Highlander was on him in a flash. He tore the phone from the boy's grasp and tossed it to Catriona. She caught it, slammed it onto the cement, and kicked the pieces into the pool.

"My *phone!*" The young man wailed as if she'd killed his twin brother.

"Before you call your lawyer, do you mind if I have you arrested as an accomplice? Maybe have your blood tested for drugs? And—related question—were you hoping to be discovered? Because you breathe a word of this to *anyone*—your mom, your therapist, the pre-pubescent psychopath on the other side of your video game headset—and you'll never work in this town again. *I promise you this.*"

The kid threw her a defiant expression, but she saw his complexion grow pale. She walked to him and stood inches from his face.

"Are we clear? Do we have an understanding?"

He set his jaw.

Tough guy. Let's try this.

"If ruining any chance of you ever having a career doesn't scare you, maybe violence will." She pointed in Broch's direction. "He's not even *close* to the biggest, scariest person I know."

The kid's gaze darted to Broch and then bounced back to her. He moved to the gate to leave.

"Fine. Tell Jax I'll call him," he muttered.

Catriona looked at Chad. "That little jerk *does* want to be famous, right?"

He nodded. "You got him dead to rights."

She called out to the boy's retreating figure. "Don't forget I know who you are—"

She shot a look at Chad, telegraphing to him that she needed a name.

"Iron Crow," he mumbled.

"Iron—*Really*?"

He nodded.

"I know who you are, *Iron Crow*." She looked around the yard. The teen girls still sat on a giant lounger, clumped in a teary group hug. "Any other witnesses?"

Chad shook his head and nodded toward Broch. "Did he hit Jax with a *rock*?"

Catriona glanced up at the balcony and saw nothing but the soles of Jaxon's feet. Broch followed her gaze.

"Did you throw a rock at him?" she asked.

"Aye."

She nodded slowly and then entered the house, Broch close on her heels. Upstairs, she checked to ensure Jaxon was breathing. He seemed fine, but for the angry, plum-sized lump on his forehead and the fact that he was unconscious.

Lot of lumpy foreheads this week.

She pulled her phone from her jeans and called Noseeum.

"Need you at Jaxon Pike's house."

"Did the little brat O.D.?"

"More of a rock to the forehead situation. That, and when he wakes up, he'll still be high on meth and who knows what else."

"Lovely. On my way."

She hung up and called Big Luther.

"Luther here."

"Tell the powers that be that Jaxon Pike will be in rehab for a while."

"*Again?*"

"Again."

"Can't Noseeum give him something to get him through this week's schedule?"

"Maybe, but that isn't going to help the huge lump on his forehead. Unless he has to wear a helmet in all his scenes this week, he's out one way or the other."

"Lump? Should I ask?"

"No."

Luther spat a string of expletives and hung up.

Catriona stood. "Our work here is done."

Broch put his hands on his hips. "Ye hae a strange job."

"No argument there. Nice throw."

He grinned. "Thank ye. Seemed the easiest way tae free the lassie."

"It didn't worry you that she might fall to her death after you knocked him unconscious?"

He scoffed. "Ah was there, wasn't ah? Ye could see she's a wee thing."

"And what if you killed *him*?"

Broch scowled at the boy. "Then he reaped whit he sowed."

She patted her intern on the arm. "Scottish justice seems a little less complicated than ours."

He put his hands on his hips. "Aye. Ah haven't seen a lot o' common sense in this place."

CHAPTER FOURTEEN

Catriona and Broch returned to her Jeep. As they hopped inside, she saw the big man put his hand against his stomach.

"Are you hungry?"

"Aye."

"I'll take you to get a Pink's hot dog. That work?"

He peered at her, his lower lip extended and the sides of his mouth downturned. "Dog?"

"A hot dog. It's not made with actual *dog*. It's beef. Cow."

He visibly relaxed. "Och, that sounds better. I lik' dogs."

"You *lick* dogs?"

He scowled. "Don't ye?"

She giggled. "Yes, I love dogs." She started the car and twisted to back up. "You don't eat hot dogs in Scotland?"

He shook his shaggy head. "If we dae, we dinnae call them that."

Catriona drove him to L.A.'s iconic hot dog stand, stealing peeks at his expression as he watched the other cars move around them. If he was pretending to be from someplace—a place without traffic—he was *good* at it.

Living in Los Angeles, she'd lost the ability to even imagine such a place.

She parked, and they walked to the bright pink building.

"What would you like on it?" she asked.

He scratched his chin. "On whit?"

"On your hot dog."

"Och—Ah dinnae ken."

She ordered him a chili bacon dog, and they found a spot to sit.

"If you don't like the stuff on top, scrape it into the trash."

He bit into the hot dog, and his eyes lit. "Ah've never had anythin' lik' this. Ye say tis made o' cow?"

She nodded, chewing her own.

"Whit part o' the cow?"

She shrugged. "Hot dogs are usually made of something between *every part* and *you don't want to know.*"

He finished the dog in a few bites and she offered to buy him another. As unorthodox as his methods had been, she felt she owed him *something* for fixing her problem with Jaxon so quickly.

He declined and finished the bottle of water she'd bought to wash down the mess, holding it up for her to see.

"That was water," he said.

She nodded, her mouth full.

"Ye *bought* water?"

She nodded again, and he shook his head in what looked like confusion, mixed with a touch of disgust.

"So, tell me about yourself. What do you do in Scotland?" she asked.

He twisted his mouth to the side as if deep in thought. "Ah think ah took care o' some wummin there. The ones wha raised me."

"You were raised by women?"

"Aye. Ah was an orphan, and they took me in."

"And you took care of their place?"

"Aye." He tilted his head as if remembering something from long ago. "And ah helped other folks in exchange fer money, tae—later."

"People hired you to help them? What did you do?"

"Ah was whit they needed. A sword, a back."

Catriona took her last bite. Sean's fascination with the stranger made more sense to her now. She wiped the mustard from her mouth. "So you were a fixer, like Sean and me? You made other people's problems go away?"

He paused and nodded. "That sounds right."

Something he'd said gnawed at the back of her brain until it occurred to her what it was.

"Wait. Did you say *sword*?"

"Aye. Mah mother Blair taught me how tae use a sword. But ah kin hunt and shoot. And ah could make food grow from"—he motioned to the paved road in front of Pink's—"from this godforsaken land."

"And how did fighting and farming bring you to Parasol Pictures' lot? I don't understand how I found you where I did."

They locked eyes, and she sensed true confusion behind his.

"You don't remember, do you?"

"Na."

"Do you remember how you got that wound in your side? Were you attacked?"

He looked away. "Ah dinnae ken."

"You dinnae ken a lot."

"Aye. Sorry—ah meant ah dinnae *know*." He overpronounced the word, imitating her American accent, and she laughed.

"Okay. We'll work on *dinnae* and *don't* later."

She crumpled napkins in her hand. Broch took it as a signal they were leaving, stood, and held out a hand to help her to her feet.

She hesitated and then took it.

"Do you want to get back home? Back to Scotland?"

"Aye." He turned and stared into her eyes. "But this place isnae *awful*."

She felt her cheeks warm. Kilty was a conundrum. She stepped back as if beholding him in his entirety would make the puzzle of him appear to her.

It did not.

"I guess I'll take you back to the lot and get you set up with your apartment," she said, avoiding his eyes.

He didn't answer but instead watched a middle-aged man approach them. His body stiffened, and he stepped between her and the stranger.

"My card," said the man, pushing a business card at Broch. "I'd love to shoot you."

Broch's chest swelled. "Aye? Dae ah get my turn at ye then?"

Catriona couldn't see Broch's expression, but the man's eyes flashed with fear. She replayed the conversation in her head and found the problem.

"He means *photograph* you, not shoot you with a *gun*," she said, touching Broch's arm. "It's all right. Just take the card."

Broch's shoulders relaxed, and he plucked the card from the man's fingers. The photographer traced the path of the scar on Broch's temple from end to end in the air two inches from the Highlander's face.

"That scar is *fascinating*. So *manly*."

Catriona couldn't be sure, but she thought she heard Broch growl.

The man glanced at Catriona, his eyes dancing with excitement.

"My *God*. If I could capture his raw sexuality on film, we'd be *millionaires*. He's got that animal magnetism thing, y'know?"

Catriona glanced at Broch.

I know.

As the photographer's attention shifted to Catriona, Broch leaned toward her as if he were blocking the stranger's view of her.

"I wouldn't hold my breath for his call if I were you," she mumbled to the man, steering Broch from the encounter.

The photographer looked Broch up and down one last time, whistled, and scurried on his way.

Broch watched him go and then turned to her. The squinty lines on either side of his eyes told her he wasn't sure the danger had passed.

"Photographs don't kill," she said, patting his bicep. "Though the bad ones can hurt for a long time."

CHAPTER FIFTEEN

Luther heard a knock, sighed, and stood from his sofa. Raising his oversized, ex-Army frame from low places grew more difficult every year.

No one had ever told him knees had a shelf-life.

Lumbering to the door, he opened it and peered at a chubby man with a lump in the middle of his forehead.

"Can I help you?"

The man smiled. "Hiya. My name's Knotty, er, *John*. John Knotty. I work for the news station, and I was wondering if you could tell me who this man is? We need to git a paper signed by him for the TV."

He held up a photo printed on paper and pointed toward a face Luther knew—two faces if he included his own. He recognized the photograph of Sean and him standing on the Parasol Pictures lot from a piece that had run on the national news. An extra had pulled a gun on set, threatening the lives of one of their stars. Luther and Sean had neutralized the threat, though the studio had spun the story to make their A-list star the hero.

He didn't mind.

Luther glowered at his smiling visitor. John Knotty's smile made him uncomfortable. It wasn't the sort of smile a person gave when bothering someone after dark. It didn't say *I'm sorry to be bothering you so late at your home.* It didn't even say, *I know* this business could wait until tomorrow, but my boss is on my back.

No. This man's smile said *don't look too closely*, and not just because one of his discolored bottom teeth had died.

"I'd like to git this paper signed. You know him?" said Knotty.

"You mean a release?"

"What?"

"This paper you want signed. It's a *release*?"

Knotty nodded. "Oh. *Right*. Yep, one of those. But we're havin' a dickens of a time finding this fella. We know he works with you, though, because there you are, next to him." He pointed at the photo.

Luther straightened to his full height of six-six and put his hands on his hips. As a rule, it was all he needed to do to encourage people to leave him alone.

"Don't you need a release from me, too?" he asked.

"Hm?" Knotty glanced at the photo and laughed. "Well, you got me. Yup."

Luther plucked the printout from Knotty's hand. "You print this out?"

"Sure."

"So, you know it's a photo of *your television.* I can see the trinkets sitting on your damn mantel. This shot of Sean and me has already *been* on television. Why do you need a release *now*?"

The man perked. "Sean? Would you happen to have his last name?"

Luther pressed his lips together and did his best to make the lumpy-headed pest melt beneath his stare. "Look, man, I don't know what you're up to, but you don't need any release. What station did you say you work for?"

"Uh, Channel Two?"

"Are you sure? You don't sound like you're *sure*."

The man dropped his cheerful façade, the corners of his mouth pressing down.

"Yep, I'm sure," he said, through gritted teeth.

Luther smirked.

Here come his true colors.

He decided to toy with the man a little longer. "You're saying you're going to rebroadcast a news clip about a problem we had at the studio *weeks* ago?" He clucked his tongue. "That's pretty poor news if you ask me."

"Yeah, well, if you could let me know how I can get hold of this Sean fella—"

Luther crumpled the paper and tossed it at the man.

"You must think I'm as dumb as you are. Get your lumpy skull off my doorstep, or I'll—"

"I wouldn't," said a new voice.

Luther looked past the chubby man to see an older man, tall, with heft to him, sporting an unkempt red beard. He held a gun in Luther's direction with a gloved hand. Something about his face seemed off-kilter like someone had taken a shovel to the lower half and knocked it out of whack.

Knotty stepped back and manifested a gun of his own.

Luther raised his hands and squared himself in the doorway.

"Look, I don't know what you two are up to—"

The red-bearded man cut him short. "Our quarrel isn't with you. Tell us where we can find Ryft, and we'll be gone."

"Rift? What's a *rift*?"

"Not a *what*, a *who*."

"He said the fella's name is Sean," offered Knotty.

"Sean what?"

"He didn't git to that part."

The bearded man snarled. "Na, ye twit, I'm asking *him*."

Before the older man could return his attention to Luther, Luther spun, bolting toward the back of his home. He heard his front door bounce off the wall as John Knotty pursued. Ripping his back door off its hinges in his haste, he burst outside and caught a split-second vision of a bat headed toward his skull.

With no time to duck, he slipped into darkness, with only one word ringing in his head.

Stupid.

CHAPTER SIXTEEN

Catriona drove Broch to the lot and walked him to the payroll office. He strolled with his long kilt tossed casually over his shoulder, winking, waving, and grinning at everyone they passed like a returning hero. Though he showed little sign of remembering, or, at least, *sharing,* any more of his mysterious past, he seemed to be warming to his new reality.

She returned him to where he'd started the day—the location of his new apartment.

The apartment located adjacent to hers.

She'd worked *years* to earn her apartment. Kilty strolled in with his muscles, rugged scars, and mysterious past and was *handed* the keys on day one.

Pfft.

A middle-aged woman with a champagne blonde bob sat behind a computer in the payroll office. She looked up as they entered and, as her gaze settled on Broch, her neck stretched and chin tucked like that of a curious bird.

"Jeanie, this is Brochan—Broch. He's going to be staying in the apartment next to mine for a while," grumbled Catriona.

Jeanie smirked. "Oh. The apartment next to yours. *Right.*"

Catriona squinted at her. "No, *seriously*. He'll be in the guest apartment, so let him up if he comes through here without me."

"You mean if you're already upstairs. Waiting. Got it."

"*No,* I mean—"

Jeanie turned her head and winked as if to hide the gesture from Broch. Unfortunately, she winked with the eye still facing him.

"Subtle, Jeanie, thanks."

"Hullo," said Broch with a little wave.

Jeanie blushed and giggled.

"No," she said, waving him away.

Catriona tugged Broch toward the elevator and opened it with her key. "We'll have to get you a spare key. I'd get it now, but only Jeanie knows where it is, and *I'm going to give her a minute to get herself together.*"

She yelled the last bit over her shoulder at the receptionist.

Broch grinned back at Jeanie.

"She seems lovely."

Jeanie melted into giggles.

Catriona rolled her eyes and guided Broch into the elevator. She shook her head, red-faced, waving to Jeanie as the doors slid shut.

They rode the elevator to the third floor, disembarked, and entered the spare apartment. The layout echoed her apartment. The studio used it as a flop spot for visitors, stars' assistants, and other emergencies.

The kitchen hadn't been updated since the late nineties, and the furniture resembled the sort left behind by a vacating fraternity. Still, the modest apartment possessed all the necessities to be comfortable.

"So, you've got your living room and kitchen here. The television probably isn't hooked up, so I hope you smuggled a good book here under your kilt."

Broch raised an eyebrow. "Ah promise ye there's no room there."

Caught off guard, she snorted a laugh, hated herself for it, and tried to hide her amusement by walking to the bedroom as he followed.

"This is the bedroom."

He tossed his long kilt on the bed and sat, bouncing up and down on it before flopping back, arms out to the side as if he'd fallen back into a pool.

"It's a *fine* kip."

"I'm glad you approve."

"Haes a lot o' give and take."

She squinted at him. "Are you *hearing* the things you're saying? I'm never sure—"

He stood and pulled his t-shirt over his head. She watched his muscles ripple over his rib cage.

Okay. *Unfair.*

Tossing the shirt on the bed, he began unsnapping his pants.

"Hey—whoa. What are you doing?" She held her palms aloft as if they would protect her from whatever might spring from his jeans. Realizing she looked like a frantic crossing guard, she closed her fingers and tried again, more calmly.

"You—you can't just start undressing here."

"I'm aff tae put mah own clothes back on. Ah cannae move in these." He hovered his hand over his crotch and winced. "Mah baws are—"

"Okay, okay, I get the idea. The jeans are tight. But you could *warn* me before you start stripping off your clothes."

"Sorry."

"You're going to put the kilt back on?"

"Aye."

He turned away from her, and she took a step toward him, pointing to the closet on the other side of the room.

"*Wait.* Do me a favor and look in the closet. We keep stuff in there for visitors. I'll try and find other clothes later. You can wear the kilt here if you *have* to, but when we're working, you have to wear *normal clothes*. One stiff breeze under your skirt, and we'll have a lawsuit on our hands."

He chuckled. "Stiff breeze."

"You're like a five-year-old."

"No, ah'm nae." He pointed at her. "*Ye* said it."

"Whatever."

He turned, and she found her face nearly nestled between his pecs. She could feel the heat rising from his chest, and her hand twitched. Her fingers wanted so badly to run across the ridges of his abs. They looked so...*touchable*—like an old-timey washboard—

Oh. That's where that comes from.

She recalled brushing the V beside his wound and silently cursed him for being so damn attractive. She wanted to reveal him as the conniving rogue he had to be, but he wouldn't stop saving people, coming to her rescue, and being so freaking *charming*.

That was the problem with handsome liars, wasn't it? They never showed you their true colors until it was too late.

Broch stared down at her with his tawny eyes, and she tried to telegraph her wishes into his brain.

Do something bad. Show me you're a con artist.

She took a deep breath, refusing to move first. He smelled like the sea. *How was that possible?* Like the sea mixed with herbs. Was that bergamot? Why was he so close?

Did I step toward him?

They'd been standing frozen, so close, for much too long.

That's when she realized what was happening.

He's going to kiss me. He's building up the nerve. He's going to grab me and kiss me, and when he does, I'm going to slap him. No— I'm going to drag my hand across his stomach first and accidentally see what that feels like, and then I'm going to slap him—

"You're mouthy for such a plain lassie," he said without shifting his blank expression.

He turned to inspect the closet, re-buttoning his jeans as he moved.

Catriona gasped as if *she'd* been slapped.

Did he just call me plain?

She cleared her throat. "I think I missed something with your accent there. It sounded like you called me *plain*."

Rooting through a pile of clothes he'd found, he glanced at her. "Aye."

"Oh—uh...What does that mean in Scottish? Is it some sort of slang?"

He scowled. "I dinnae think sae. It means *plain*. Nothing

fancy."

She pointed to the center of her chest and opened her mouth, but no sound escaped. She'd been called many things in her time, but *plain* had never been one of them. A boy had once called her *sporty* in a mean tone, but she'd taken that as a compliment—and proof he was an idiot.

She scoffed.

"The women in Scotland must be *amazing* because I'll have you know there is no shortage of men around here who don't think I'm *plain. And we're in L.A.*"

She cringed.

She sounded *so* obnoxious.

Why did I say that?

He straightened, flipping out a folded pair of jeans he'd found. "Ye don't say?"

"I *do* say. Some fairly famous actors and stuntmen and—" She swirled a finger in his direction. "Men every bit as hard and strong and *bulgy* as you, say so, too."

She slapped her hand over her mouth.

Now he's making me repeat this obnoxiousness. Someone shut me up.

He grunted and held up the jeans. "Ye think these will fit me?"

She crossed her arms against her chest, her jaw set. "I—"

She cut herself short. *No. Don't say another word.* She threw up her chin, lips puckered in the hopes she could keep them shut.

He tilted his head. "Were ye aff tae say something?"

No, don't fall for it. Don't you dare.

"It sounded lik' ye were aboot tae say somethin'?" he urged again.

She shook her head and heard the words explode from her mouth.

"What's so wrong with me? I suppose I'm not girly enough for you, huh? Nails not long enough? Heels not high enough?"

Now it was his turn to cross his arms and squint at her. He stared at her for a good minute. She wanted to smack him. Or run. Be anywhere, but standing there feeling as stupid as she did at that moment. If he thought she was plain, that was *fine*. That was his prerogative, crazy as it might be. But her defensive reaction to it—she wanted to crawl under the bed.

He scratched his chin and nodded as if he were a detective making an important deduction. "Ye know, ah think yer accusin' me of somethin', but the way ye said that word—*girly*—it sounds tae me lik' *yer* the one with a problem with the lassies. What's wrong with bein' girly?"

She scowled. "What? There's nothing wrong with being girly. I meant you're intimidated by my *confidence*. Like you'd prefer I wear frilly dresses maybe? Be a bit meeker—"

He walked toward her, and she refused to fall back.

The idea that this swaggering animal thinks he can intimidate me—

His hand moved toward her hip.

She flinched but held her ground. She mentally ran through her checklist of ways she'd *destroy his world* if he tried to hurt her before a calm washed over her.

He's not going to hurt me.

She smirked.

It's a joke. I get it now. He's going to kiss me. He's slipping his hand behind my back to pull me tight. He thinks he's some romantic hero about to sweep me—

Instead of reaching behind her, he encircled her wrist with his index finger and thumb and gently pulled it forward. He laid her hand flat, palm down, against his upturned palm. Her hand looked dainty in his great paw. She'd never considered her fingers particularly dainty before.

"Yer nails are painted," he said.

Her focus adjusted to the tips of her nails painted in a muted coral tone.

"So?"

"So, that's *girly*, isnae it?"

She blinked at him. "I suppose. *So?*"

He put his other hand over hers. "Ye said mah problem with ye, is that yer nae girly enough fer me. But you're girly enough noo, aren't ye?"

She stared at him, dumbfounded.

He smiled, white teeth flashing against his dark stubble. "Not girly enough? Na. Ah guess that's nae it."

He booped the tip of her nose with his finger.

"*Oooh.*" She growled, ripping her hand from his.

While planning a scathing retort, she heard the elevator doors open. Quaking with anger, she shook a fist at the brute like some sort of nineteen-fifties television character and pounded into the main living area.

She found Sean standing in the living room, a book in his hands.

"What are you doing here?" she asked.

"I hope I'm not interrupting anything. You look flushed."

She cleared her throat and jerked her thumb in the direction of the bedroom. "Of course not. I'm showing Kilty MacJackass his new apartment."

Sean chuckled. "Sounds like the two of you are getting along splendidly."

Broch entered the room bare-chested but wearing new, well-fitting jeans. He brushed past her.

"Hello again, sir," he said, shaking Sean's hand.

"*Hello again, sir,*" she echoed in a barely audible, mocking tone. She caught Sean's gaze and motioned to Kilty.

"Sorry. He's still struggling with the whole *wearing clothes* thing."

Sean clapped Broch on the arm as if he were an old war buddy. "I see you found some better jeans. Good. Oh, and I heard you did a heck of a job with that terror, Jaxson."

Catriona scoffed. "Yeah, *rocks* are the answer to all our problems. Who knew?" She glared at the ground, took a cleansing breath, and then looked back up at Sean. "Anyway, what are you doing here? Is something wrong?"

Sean arched an eyebrow. "You think the only time I come to town is when something's wrong?"

She held his gaze.

"Fair enough. You have a point." He held up the book in his

hand. She now saw it was a composition notebook with the classic speckled black and white cover. "I've thought about this long and hard, and I've decided it's time I shared some things with you. I was going to hold off, but—I want you to read this." He held out the book.

"What is it?"

"Just some notes. A sort of hasty personal history, most of which you already know, but…"

Catriona looked at him, but his gaze darted away.

"Why don't you just *tell* me what it is you want me to know?" she asked.

He dismissed her comment by shaking the book. "This is easier."

She took it. "Why now? Why in front of *him*?"

"You'll see. I have to go. I have a meeting. I'll talk to you when I get back. Just read it."

He nodded to each of them and turned to leave.

After a single step, her adoptive father paused and made a one-eighty to face her. For a moment, it appeared he didn't know what to do.

Then, he did the oddest thing.

He threw his arms around her and hugged her tight.

"What's this for?" she asked as the air squeezed from her lungs.

"I need a reason to hug my girl?" he asked.

He released her, and she was struck by how much his eyes reminded her of Broch's, fawn in color, flecked with stars of a darker brown.

He winked and looked past her at Broch. "Take care of her."

Broch nodded. "Aye."

Sean walked into the hallway and entered the waiting elevator. The doors closed.

Catriona looked down at the book in her hand.

"I'm going to go back to my place. It's right next door if you need anything."

Broch nodded, and she headed down the hallway to her apartment, holding the book tight against her chest.

Nothing felt right.

CHAPTER SEVENTEEN

The floors creaked.

Broch sat up.

Catriona stood at the foot of his bed, holding the book Sean had given her in the air like a weapon. Wet, scraggly hair clung to her cheeks. His hair was damp as well. He'd discovered the shower and had found it *impossible* to leave the gloriously warm water until it turned cold.

"Did *you* make him write this?" she asked, her voice high and strained.

"Eh?" He gathered the sheet to cover himself. The glowing box on the nightstand beside him said it was three o'clock in the morning. He glanced at it, noted the time, and then found it hard to pull his gaze away from the red numbers.

Glowing time.

What a place the world has become.

"This nonsense about time travel—It's you, isn't it?" she asked.

He turned his attention back to Catriona.

Lassie looks mad.

Again.

He had an inkling of what had riled her but chose not to respond for fear he'd guess wrong. That would be like handing an unarmed person a weapon.

She pointed at him, and even in the dim light, he could see

her eyes aflame with fury, welling with what he read as tears of frustration. He closed his eyes.

"Dinnae cry. Ah cannae bear it."

"He's losing his mind, and you took advantage of him," she said, her voice shaky.

"Wha?"

"Sean."

Broch held up his hands. "Na. T'is nae whit ye mind, lassie. We discussed our—*time problem*—but nothing more. Tis *him* what tellt *me*."

"He *tellt* you what?"

"That he's come here fae the past. As we believe ah hae."

Catriona's nose wrinkled as if he was the most terrible thing she'd ever seen. He understood her confusion; he, too, grappled with what Sean had told him. He didn't know how to make her believe the crazy story he'd come to believe was true. Trying to make her believe might make everything worse for her. The conversation he'd had with Sean by the pool had certainly done little to make *him* feel better.

"Listen. This mornin' when ah went oot tae bathe—"

She scoffed. "You know swimming isn't the same as bathing, right?" She glanced at the book. "Oh, I get it. That's something a guy from the eighteenth century would do, isn't it? Bathe in a pool. *Nice try.* Pretending you didn't know what a phone was, wearing that stupid kilt—it's all part of your plan, isn't it?"

"Whit *plan*?"

"Sean doesn't have any money, you know. Do you think he does? Did—*wait*—was this all a ruse to get a job on the lot? Are you trying to get discovered? Are you a paparazzi?"

He stood and tied the sheet around his waist. "A dinnae ken whit yer sayin'—"

"Oh no?" She opened the book and flipped through the pages before reading aloud. *"I can only assume Brochan is my darling babe, saved from the fire by the Broken Women for whom I'd happily done many a chore."*

"Whit's that noo?" Broch strode forward as best he could

with the sheet dragging from his waist and took the book from her hands. He re-read the passage.

"Sean minds he's mah da?"

"*Yes*, because that's what you tried to *make* him think—"

She jerked the book from his hands, and he pounded an invisible table with his fist. "*Na.* This isnae a thing ah've done. Ah tellt him whit ah remembered and he tellt me the same happened tae him. He said it's whit our people dae."

"*What your people do?*" Catriona paced toward the kitchen, her hand on her head, muttering to herself. "He must be losing his mind." She poked her head back into the bedroom. "And if you're not *evil*, then you're losing your mind, too."

She disappeared a second time.

He shuffled after her as fast as the sheet would allow, feeling like a landed fish.

"He isnae losing his mind," he said.

"How can you say that? You talked him into believing the two of you traveled through time. That you're his *son*."

"Ah *dinnae*. He made *me* believe it."

"You're up to something."

As she spoke, she chopped the air with the notebook to punctuate her words. Something flew from between the pages and fluttered to the ground between them. They locked eyes, frozen, before both dove to retrieve it. Catriona reached it first and spun away with it in her hand.

She scurried behind the kitchen island to create a barrier between them, studying the object, and then flipped over the square to inspect the other side.

"Is this a joke?" she asked, though some of the vinegar seemed to have drained from her.

"Whit?"

She thrust it toward him. It was a square piece of paper with a picture of a man sitting on the hood of a car, smiling. Broch stared at it for some time. He recognized the man in the photo from every reflective object he'd ever gazed into.

He turned to Catriona for answers.

"Tis me?"

"Certainly looks like it."

"Howfur kin that be?"

She chewed at her lip. "I don't know. Thing is, I recognize the car. It's Sean's old Jaguar. That's *him*—and he looks like *you*."

"The drawing is very fine," he said, running his hand over the image.

She rolled her eyes. "It's a *photo*."

Brock frowned. Pulling from her pocket the little black box she always kept near, she pointed it at him. It was the same sort of device she'd asked him to take from the boy—what had she called it?

A phone.

The boy looked as though he *died* when she kicked his phone into the pool.

Catriona flipped the phone for him to see the other side.

Inside the little black box, Broch found a glowing picture of himself. He looked behind him to confirm the things in the photo—the top of the sofa, the wall—were the things behind him now.

He didn't know what to say.

"You look baffled." She ran a hand through her hair and tilted her head back to stare at the ceiling. "None of this can be possible."

Catriona's face twitched as though she were experiencing a thousand emotions at once. After a moment, her eyes flashed white, and she pointed at him. "You're a *terrible* person."

She sounded less angry, and more like she was trying to *convince* herself she was angry.

Broch returned his attention to the photo.

"Yer telling me this is Sean as a young man?" he asked.

"Yes. If he isn't your father, you're his evil twin from another dimension."

"His evil—?"

She shook her head. "It's a joke. I'm saying he *must* be your father. I don't know. This is *insane*. I don't want to believe it. I can't—"

Broch fell silent. His mothers never told him the identity of his father or how the man died.

Could it be Sean was his father? That he, too, had traveled to this place?

Catriona paced. "Let's say all this is true. Let's say you've come here through time from—what year was it for you last you remember?"

"Seventeen forty-nine."

"Wow. Okay. Seventeen forty-nine. Let's say Sean traveled here—"

"Howfur?"

Her brow knit. "*What*?"

"Howfur he traveled? Did the book tellt?"

"It said he thought you and your mother were dead. How did *you* travel?"

"Ah dinnae ken. Ah dinnae dae it on purpose."

"Right. Naturally. Do you ever ken *anything*?"

He shrugged.

"What do you remember? Did the women—your mothers—tell you anything about your family?"

"Na. They said it would be dangerous tae tell me who ah was."

Catriona held up the finger of one hand and used the other to hold up her phone and speak into it.

"You're talking tae my picture?" he asked. He cocked his head to listen if her voice seemed as close to his ear as her lips were to his image.

"What? *No*. I'm searching for the name Thorn Campbell."

He nodded. He had no idea what she was talking about, but if anyone was losing their mind, it was probably the poor lassie.

Her voice trailed off, and she stared intently at the phone. "Did you say your family was from Glenorchy?"

"Aye."

"There's a legend about a guy named Thorn Campbell. It says in seventeen twenty-one he had it in for Rob Roy MacGregor's right-hand man—a guy named Ryft." She looked up. "That's the name Thorn asked me about."

"Aye." He raised an eyebrow. "That picture box is telling ye that?"

She held up the phone, and he saw the front of it was now covered with words.

Witchcraft.

"Tis a book noo." He scratched at his chin, studying it. "Can ah get one of those?"

She rolled her eyes and continued reading. A moment later, she gasped.

"What's it tellin' ye noo?"

"Thorn burned Ryft's wife, Isobel, and their baby to death in their home, and then the two men fought—and during the battle, they both disappeared in a strange fog, never to be heard from again."

"When ah tellt Sean aboot the women wha raised me, he asked if ah had a mother named Isobel."

"Did you?"

"Na, nae that ah knew, but—" In his mind's eye, Broch pictured a single word stamped into the leather of his saddle. "Mah mothers gave me a saddle ah mind they dinnae have the money tae buy. It had a name on it."

"Don't tell me—"

He nodded. "Aye. *Ryft.*"

Catriona's jaw fell.

"The name didnae mean anything tae me. Ah wasnae even sure Ryft t'was a name. But noo—"

"Thorn is looking for Ryft, and *Sean is Ryft.*"

"And mah father."

"And all three of you are from the seventeen hundreds." Catriona placed her hand on her forehead as if she were feeling for a fever. "This is *insane.* It's *impossible.* Yet, everything's connecting—"

Broch paced. "But why am ah here? Maybe ah'm here tae protect mah father?"

Catriona gasped a second time, and Broch stopped pacing.

"Whit t'is it noo?"

She looked panicked. "We have to *go.* We have to find Sean."

"Whitfur?"

"That *hug*. I know him. He left us the book, so we'd know the truth if he *didn't come back*. He's gone after Thorn. We have to help him."

Broch held up his palm, attempting to calm her. "Keep the heid noo."

She was already across the room on her way to the door when she stopped and turned.

"What did you say?"

"Whit?"

"What did you just say?"

He took a moment to recall.

"Keep the heid?"

She pointed a finger at him and took a step forward. "Why did you say *that*?"

"Uh...fur ah wanted ye tae keep the heid? To settle?"

He could see her body trembling and felt overwhelmed by the urge to hold her. She was such a strong lassie. It hurt him to see her so shaken.

"Lassie, whit is it?"

She swallowed. "Sean says that."

"He says *keep the heid*?"

She nodded. "He's been telling me that my whole life. Did you hear it from him?"

He shook his head. "Na."

"It's something they say in Glenorchy?"

"Aye. It's—" He cut short, worried what he'd remembered would upset her.

"It's what?"

He sighed. "My mothers said my father always said it tae them. They'd call him, upset aboot one thing or another, and he'd say *Keep the heid, wummin!* And they'd all roar with laughter, and it wid make them feel better."

Catriona looked away. "This is too much."

"Aye. Look—" Broch took a step toward her. The wound on his side ached. He winced.

"You came with a stab wound," she said.

He stopped. "Sae?"

"Well, if the legend is true and Sean and Thorn were transported to modern-day while fighting, maybe you were, too. Do you remember anything like that?"

Broch suffered a flash of a memory—a man in dark clothing and pain in his side like he'd been bitten by a dragon.

Not enough to mention.

He shook his head. "Na."

She motioned to his side. "Let me see it."

"My wound?"

"Yes. It probably needs to be re-bandaged."

He shook his head. "Ah dinnae ken... Ye was terrible mad at me a moment ago. Might nae be a good idea tae let ye poke around mah tender flesh quite yet."

She chuckled, and he thought he caught a touch of color rising to her cheeks.

"I'm sorry I yelled. I'm frustrated. None of this makes sense. I'm worried about Sean. I—"

She paused as if she were afraid to continue.

"Ye were feart ah was workin' with Thorn?"

She nodded and picked up the photo.

"This picture. It's impossible, but I can't explain it. Every new piece of information supports this crazy time-traveling idea. If I'm honest with myself, you *do* seem out of your time. Unless you're just an amazing actor."

He grinned. "Ah'll be honest with ye. Ah've never been good at pretendin' ah'm anyone but who ah am. And that haesnae always been good fer me."

A silence fell between them, and she nodded toward his hip. "The wound."

"Och. Aye, then. Ah'll trust ye."

She approached, and he moved the sheet enough to reveal the wound. The bandage was stained with blood.

She knelt beside him to pull away the sticky wrapping. It hurt as it released from his flesh, and he looked away so she wouldn't see him wince.

"Yer good at tendin'. You have a gentle touch." It was a bit of a lie, but he did appreciate the effort.

"Thanks. It looks better. Did you use the antibiotic?"

"Aye. Though ah still dinnae understand whatfer."

She chuckled. "I think it's too early in the morning for me to explain bacteria to you." She cocked her head. "To be honest, I'm not sure I *could*. That might require more googling."

He brushed a lock of hair sliding close to her eye away.

"Ah'm wantin' ye tae ken—er, *know*—ah'm nae here tae hurt ye. Ah'll help ye find Sean. If whit he says in the book is true, he's someone who's been on mah mind mah whole life. Ah cannae let him slip away from me, just as ah've found him."

She looked up at him, and he put his hand beneath her chin to hold her gaze to his own.

"Tell me ye ken ah willnae hurt ye."

She sighed and closed her eyes.

"I believe you."

CHAPTER EIGHTEEN

Sean retrieved his cell phone and dialed. Tommy Hopkins, a man he and Catriona often used for surveillance and other feet-on-the-ground operations, answered.

"You have eyes on Thorn?" he asked.

"He's at his hotel with two men. I sent you the info."

"Any background?"

Tommy sighed. "Thorn Campbell has been living in Tennessee as a mid-level drug runner—OxyContin mostly. Been at it for decades."

Sean grunted. "Thanks. Stay on him."

He hung up.

Found him.

The red-bearded fiend had holed up in a cheap hotel on the outskirts of town with his two henchmen. Sean didn't understand how the man had appeared after all these years, or how he'd found Catriona.

If Brochan hadn't been there—

Sean took a deep breath.

Brochan.

My boy.

His throat tightened at the thought of reuniting with the babe he thought he'd lost so long ago. He'd found his home burned to ashes, his wife's body blackened. There'd been no sign of his infant son, but the fire had been fierce. There'd been no reason to believe the child survived. Blinded by rage and pain, he'd left to exact his revenge on Thorn.

Remembering that terrible day, Sean lay his hand on his abdomen, beneath his ribs. The last time he'd seen Thorn, they'd been locked in battle. He'd heard someone call out for their *da*, and—his lost newborn boy weighing heavy on his mind—he'd turned. He'd lost focus for a precious moment.

Thorn ran him through.

That's when Sean jumped. He had to. Time travel erased old age and healed injuries—except those caused by another Traveler.

Those wounds took much longer to heal.

Luckily, Thorn was a common man. He hadn't left a scar—not on Sean's physical body. But, somehow, Thorn must have been pulled forward in time with him, bound to him by that sword.

In seventeen twenty-one, Sean had a woman he loved, a cause to fight for, a child—

Now, he was driving a car in the twenty-first century, looking for his ancient enemy.

No time to spend in the past now.

He couldn't wait for Thorn Campbell to snatch Catriona again. He couldn't wait for the bastard to find Brochan or knock on his door. The time had come to end the feud between them once and for all.

Time to avenge sweet Isobel.

Sean fought the urge to wallow in regret.

If only I'd known.

Thorn had been in Tennessee for *decades*. The bastard had found his bearings, learned the modern world, and used modern weapons.

I've lost my chance to surprise him.

Sean's phone buzzed. A text.

911.

He reached onto the passenger seat to grab his phone. The text was from Luther. The phone buzzed again.

Another 911.

Not good.

Two exits from Luther's, Sean stepped on the gas and pulled off the freeway.

He coasted to a stop half a block from Luther's home. No lights glowed in the windows of his friend and co-worker's home.

Sean turned off his engine and headed for the house. A shadow paralleled the edge of Luther's front door.

The door was open.

Sean crept toward the porch, gun drawn.

Easing the door open a few more inches, he peered into the darkness, allowing his eyes to adjust.

No movement inside, but there was *sound.*

Breathing.

A heartbeat.

He sensed someone behind the door, waiting for him to enter.

Sean slammed his shoulder into the door and heard an expelling of breath as his enemy was crushed against the wall. The man's hand thrust out, his fingers wrapped around a gun. Sean grabbed his wrist and pounded it against the wall until the weapon clattered to the floor.

Sensing another movement behind him, Sean gave the door a last slam into the first man's skull. He whirled as he squatted, one leg out, sweeping across the ankle of his new attacker. The man yelped and flipped on his side like a diner pancake. Sean pounced, striking him hard in the throat. Gagging, the man dropped his gun and clawed at his throat, gasping for breath.

Sean stood to finish the man crawling out from behind the door.

That's when he heard the shotgun pump.

A light in the kitchen flickered on to reveal an old man.

Age didn't matter.

Sean recognized Thorn Campbell.

Thorn's shotgun leveled at Sean's chest. He held the weapon with one hand, finger on the trigger, stock pressed against his chest. When he spoke, his jaw clicked in and out of place, giving his speech a strange, additional cadence.

"Hello Ryft, I see ye haven't forgotten how to fight."

Sean's shoulders released. "And I see you're as good-looking as ever."

Thorn laughed a slow, menacing chuckle. "I saw your boy. He just arrive?"

Sean shook his head. "I don't know what you're talking about."

"Sure ye don't."

The kitchen light revealed more than Thorn's crooked face. Behind him, crawling across the linoleum floor, Luther appeared—his facial features swollen and eyes barely more than slits.

Sean guessed Thorn's men had worked him over and left him for dead.

That was a mistake.

Luther was one of the toughest men Sean had ever known, and he'd known a few.

In the kitchen, Luther reached up and slid his phone from the table. Sean looked away to keep Thorn from spotting the flash of recognition on his face.

Sean heard the man behind him groan as he dragged himself from behind the door. The man would have a similar line of sight and might spot Luther as he crawled back into the kitchen.

He couldn't let that happen.

The other man, the one lying at Sean's feet, tried to sit up. Sean kicked him in the side of the head, knocking him out cold. Whirling, he backhanded the man behind him with a closed fist, sending him stumbling against the wall.

Sean felt confident his attacker wouldn't see Luther from his new vantage point—tangled in a potted palm.

"Stop!" roared Thorn. "I'll *kill* ye if you don't put your hands in the air."

Sean faced him. "Sorry. I don't know what came over me."

"That'll be enough out of you."

Sean felt cold steel at the base of his neck. The man in the palm must have worked his way free.

Sean peered into the kitchen.

No sign of Luther.

The man jerked Sean's arms back, securing them with a zip tie.

Thorn took a step forward. "I didn't know what to make of your boy when I saw him, Sean. It was like seeing your ghost. I froze. I did. Spitting image of you, isn't he?"

Sean remained stone-faced.

Thorn continued, leering. "Then it hit me. I was looking at your *son*." He laughed. "I thought it might be fun to kill him in front of you—what do you think? Maybe his girl, too. I wonder if she'll squeal the way your Isobel did?"

Sean felt his body spasm with rage. He lunged forward, but the man behind him held his arms and kicked him in the back of the knees until he folded.

Thorn grinned his horrible, crooked smile.

"I'd like to kill them both. Right here in front of you. *Right now*. But I don't want to be stuck in this godforsaken town for months huntin' them down. I think if your boy knows I have his daddy, he'll come runnin' to *me*—don't you?"

Sean's lip curled. "Look me in the eye, Thorn. Look at me and know *this face* is the last thing you'll ever see before I send you straight to hell."

Thorn smirked and, looking past Sean, nodded.

Something struck Sean in the back of the head, and he slipped into darkness.

CHAPTER NINETEEN

Catriona opened her eyes and realized she'd fallen asleep on the Highlander's shoulder. She'd been eager to find Sean but had no idea where to start. She and Kilty sat on the sofa to discuss the possibilities of Sean's whereabouts and the improbabilities of time travel. She remembered letting her head fall back and closing her eyes for what she thought would be a second.

Now the sun was up.

Brochan sat to her right, and a blanket lay draped over her.

She leaned forward and noticed Broch's eyes were open.

"We fell asleep," she said.

"Aye. It took all mah energy tae keep ye fae running oot into the night wi'oot a plan."

She stood, folded the blanket, and placed it on the back of the sofa. "I suppose you gave me this. Thank you."

He shrugged.

Broch stood, adjusted his sheet skirt, and scratched his fingers across his bare chest. "Tis morn."

Catriona found her phone and dialed Sean again. The phone went to voicemail, and she dropped it on the sofa, disgusted with it.

"I still can't reach him."

"Ah dinnae think twas his plan tae be reached."

"That's what I'm afraid of. We need to find Big Luther. If anyone knows something, it will be him. Sean wouldn't plan a trip to the donut shop without him."

"Aye. Ah need but a moment."

Broch strode into the bedroom, and she heard the shower come to life.

She moved to the bedroom.

"What are you doing?" she called as she entered.

The door to the bathroom was open. She could see the shape of his body through the frosted glass of the shower. His eyes peered over the top of the enclosure.

"Ah'm bathin'. See? Ah figured it oot. Not the pool, this here."

"Now? I thought we were going?"

He raised his arms and rubbed the soap in his armpit. "It'll only tak' a wee moment. Last night, afore ye came over, ah found this cake o' sweet-smelling soft stone—like what mah mothers used."

"Soap. It's *soap*. Hey—" She'd turned to leave and then turned back. "Did you say you were in the shower last night?"

"Aye."

She huffed. "That explains why I had to take a *cold* shower. I thought something was wrong with the pipes. You used up all the hot water."

"Ah dinnae ken it could run oot." He groaned with what sounded like ecstasy. "The water is sae warm. Ah kin make it hotter, tae. 'Til ah kin barely *stand* it."

"Amazing. You're a time traveler *and* a wizard."

He finished rinsing and opened the door.

Catriona spun her back to his naked body. "Could you maybe have an *ounce* of humility?"

A voice whispered in her ear, breath hot on her neck. "A*h* am a wizard. Ah've come through time to enchant ye."

She jumped and slapped her hand to her chest. He had to have scampered across the floor like a mouse to reach her so quickly and quietly.

Catriona kept her back to him, and his fingers appeared, waggling on either side of her skull, teasing. She slapped one hand away. He circled, and as soon as she caught a glimpse of his torso, she shut her eyes.

"Broch, for the love of—"

"Dinnae ye want to see mah wizard's wand?"

She exploded with laughter that made her cover her face and turn away from him again. The last thing she wanted to do was encourage his shenanigans, but he'd caught her off-guard.

"Look, you Scottish freak—this is serious. Sean might be in trouble. Will you get dressed and stop acting like a two-year-old?"

"Open yer eyes."

"No."

"Open yer eyes."

"*No.*"

He lightly tickled her sides, and she spun, hands balled into fists.

"I don't know who you think—" She barked her shin against the bench at the foot of the bed and yelped, eyes springing open.

Broch stood before her in jeans, his hands outspread like he'd nailed the landing.

"Ah'm dressed. See? Ah'm magic. Ah tol' ye."

She hobbled out of the room. "You still need a shirt, idiot."

"Ye people are crazy aboot yer shirts, aren't ye?" he called after her.

Catriona perched herself on the kitchen bar stool, rubbing at her shin.

"Once we find Sean, you can move to an island somewhere and run around naked all day."

He appeared from the bedroom, pulling on a new tee over his head. "Ah'm gonna hold ye tae that promise."

He winked.

The tee had a picture of a chicken on it. Above the chicken hung the phrase: *Guess What?* with an arrow pointing to the chicken's butt.

She covered her face with her hand.

"Why would you pick that shirt?"

"It haes a chicken on it. Guess whit ah had on mah farm?"

"Chickens?"

He grinned and pointed at her. "Aye."

"But that shirt doesn't say *Guess What? Chicken.* It says *Guess What? Chicken Butt.*"

He peered down at the tee. "Whatfur?"

"It rhymes. It's something kids say. They ask someone *Guess what?* and then when the person says *What?* they say *Chicken butt!* and burst out laughing."

He laughed.

Catriona squinted at him. "You know, you're not *half* as charming as you think you are."

He pursed his lips and looked up as if considering her comment. After posing like that for a moment, he shook his head.

"Na. Ah am. Ah'm sure of it."

He walked past her and out of the apartment.

Catriona scowled.

He smells really good.

They drove to Big Luther's house and saw the ambulance and police lights from blocks away.

Catriona stomped on the gas until official vehicles blocked her path and she was forced to stop, tires squealing for mercy. She spilled out of the car and wove through the small crowd of people who'd gathered to watch the excitement. After waiting for a policeman to look the other way, she dipped beneath the crime tape and dodged another officer who tried to stop her from entering the scene.

She spotted Luther in the back of the ambulance parked in front of his home. He lifted his head to peer at her, his face bloodied and swollen.

"Luther! What happened? Are you okay? Have you seen Sean?"

He waved a massive paw at her. "It's all right, Kitty Cat, don't get yourself in a lather. Sean was here. Three men took him when they heard the sirens."

An EMT held out his arm, blocking her from entering the ambulance.

"Miss, I'm going to have to ask you to leave." The EMT tried to ease her away. She balked. She was about to snap at the man for making an already stressful situation more difficult when she felt something move behind her.

A shadow fell across the bumper of the emergency vehicle. The EMT cut short and stared past her, eyes widening.

She hooked a thumb toward the object of his fascination.

"A big guy is standing behind me, isn't he?"

The EMT nodded.

"The lassie needs a moment," said Broch.

The EMT grimaced. "But—"

"A *moment*," insisted Broch.

The EMT sighed. "Fine. Make it quick."

"I'm sorry," said Catriona, hoping her eyes telegraphed her good intentions. The EMT was only doing his job, but she had to gather more information.

She turned her attention to Luther.

"Who were the three men? What did they look like?"

Luther raised his head again and winced with the few parts of his face that weren't stretched tight by swollen bruises. "Never saw them before. Big, older guy with a red beard, skinny younger guy, and a hefty guy with a—"

She cut him short. "Lump on his forehead."

"Yeah. You know them?"

"We've met. You say they *took* Sean?"

Luther nodded. "He gave them a run for their money, but yeah, they got him in the end. I was in no shape. They got me good before he showed up."

"Okay. Take care, Luther. I'll let the studio know."

He grabbed her wrist. "Call my niece, Tanya. Do you have her number?"

"I do. Will do. Don't worry about a thing."

"Right." Luther lay his head back down and raised his fingers without moving his arm to wave.

"Sorry," she said again to the EMT.

Gaze avoiding Broch, the technician nodded and closed the ambulance's doors.

Catriona's stomach roiled with nerves as she strode back to her Jeep.

"I don't know enough about these men to know where they'd take him."

Her phone rang and she pulled it from her pocket to see Sean's name.

"*Sean*," she answered.

Broch's attention snapped to her.

No one spoke on the other side of the line.

"Sean? I can't hear you. Are you there?"

She covered her opposite ear with her hand and walked away from the crowd. She heard only heavy breathing.

"Who is this now?" said a rough voice.

Her face prickled as the blood drained from it.

"Who is *this*? Why do you have this phone?" she asked.

The man chuckled. "You're the girl, aren't you? I recognize that mouth of yours. The man has half a dozen numbers on his phone, and you're one of them. I guess you knew Ryft after all."

Thorn. She'd expected as much.

"What do you want?"

"It's not about what I want. It's about what *you* want. If you want to see Sean alive again, you're going to wait a few days, and then I'm going to tell ye where you can find him."

"Why are you doing this?"

"You don't know?" Thorn chuckled again. "You never told her who you are?" he said, his voice farther away as if he'd turned his head from the phone. "Your own—daughter?"

"Thorn, talk to me," said Catriona.

Thorn grunted. "You remember my name. How nice. A few days. I'll call. And bring the Highlander with you, or no deal."

"Wait—"

The phone went dead.

"Whit t'is it?" asked Broch.

Before she could answer, her phone rang again. The caller ID announced the Los Angeles Police department.

She answered. "Hello?"

"Hello, is this Catriona Phoenix?" asked a woman.

"Yes."

"Miss, this is Detective Dolan from the L.A. Police Department. Do you know a Tommy Lee Hopkins?"

Catriona scowled, recognizing the name of the man both she and Sean used for various errands—usually those of the less legal sort.

"Why? Is he in trouble?"

"Is he your boyfriend? Husband?"

"*Friend.* Can I ask what this is about?"

"Miss, we found your number on his phone. I'm going to need you to come in, or I can send an officer to pick you up."

Catriona closed her eyes. This was the last thing she needed.

"Can you tell me what's going on first?" she asked.

She heard the officer sigh and could tell she was either weighing the pros and cons of sharing more information with her or bracing herself to deliver bad news.

"Miss," began the officer before a lengthy pause. "I'm sorry to have to tell you, but Mr. Hopkins is dead."

CHAPTER TWENTY

"Where are we now?" asked Broch as he sat in Catriona's car. He gazed through the window. A few days ago, he didn't even know what a car was. Now, it seemed he couldn't live without one.

He glanced at Catriona. Her jaw was set and taut. Her hands gripped the wheel, though they were parked in front of a low, long building.

She'd looked like a woman possessed ever since speaking to Thorn on the phone. Her family friend was beaten bloody, Sean had been taken, and another friend had died.

It frustrated Broch. He had *no idea* how to help her other than to stay near and wait for a moment to see where he'd be useful.

"Are ye all richt?" he asked.

"Oh, I'm great," she muttered. "Why?"

"Och. Na reason. Except it looks lik' you're aboot tae snap either that wheel or yer own fingers."

She released the steering wheel and wrung her hands together. "The police said Tommy was found dead in his car up on that ridge," she said, pointing toward a low outcropping of land, topped by a fence and what looked like another parking lot. "He doesn't live anywhere near here. I think he was watching this motel, and I think I know why."

"Motel? Is that—"

"You'd know it as a *lodge*, I guess."

"No, I ken the French word *hotel*. Ah tol ye ah ken some French. It's the *m* confusing me."

She blinked at him. "You really do know French?"

He grinned. "Ah tol ye ah'm not as dumb as ah look."

He slid a sideward glance at her and saw her smile. Mission accomplished. He'd cheered her up, even if it was only for a moment.

She pointed at the motel. "I never said you were *dumb*. People stay in these less fancy hotels during road trips. *Motel* is a combination of hotel and motor—motors are the things in the cars that make them move."

"Ah. From the Latin *motor* which means *mover*."

She snorted a laugh. "Okay, now you're just showing off."

Catriona got out of the car, and Broch followed.

"Ye think Thorn and his men are staying here? Sean had this *Tommy* watching them?"

"Yes." She headed toward a door marked *Office*. "They've probably left, but it's a place to start."

He nodded. "Shouldn't we hae weapons?"

"I have my gun."

He scowled. "*Ah* dinnae have a gun."

"It's okay. I'm sure they're gone. I could hear they were in a car on the phone. They're headed somewhere they think is safe. I need to figure out where that is, and the motel might have information on them."

"Och." Broch grinned. "You're not as stupid as you look either."

She glared at him and entered the motel to the tune of a jingling bell. Inside, she approached a man standing behind a desk and pulled a wallet from her pocket.

"Hello, sir, my name is Detective Cathy Jones, and I work with the L.A. homicide division." She opened and shut the wallet quickly, flashing the contents to the man, who immediately grew paler. His eyes drifted to Broch to look him up and down. Broch drew himself to his full height and puffed out his chest.

Catriona glanced at his Chicken Butt tee shirt and looked

away, shaking her head.

"We're undercover," she added.

The clerk nodded. "How can I help you, detectives?"

"You had some men staying here we believe are connected to a murder that happened nearby. Does the name Thorn Campbell ring a bell?"

The man shook his head.

Broch held his hands out to mock a large belly. "Big guy. Looks lik' me if ah ate three more of me."

The clerk stared at him.

"Big red beard," added Catriona.

The man's eyes grew wide. "Oh. I remember *him*."

"When did he leave?"

He shrugged. "Don't know for sure, but he paid up last night. Said he was leaving early for Tennessee to get *the hell out of this godforsaken town*." The clerk chuckled at the memory.

"Did he pay by credit card?" asked Catriona.

"Cash."

"Has his room been cleaned?"

"Oh, yes. We pride ourselves on our clean rooms."

"Did you scan his driver's license or—"

"He put his license plate down here." The man bent down to retrieve a box of registration cards. Ruffling through, he found the one he wanted and plucked it out. "The man he had with him, a thin man, he wrote his name and license plate here."

Catriona took the card and handed it to Broch. "We're going to take this for a bit."

"Okay. No problem. Do you want me to call you if I see him again?"

Catriona was already turning to leave. "What? Oh, yes."

Again she tried to go, but the man called after her. "Do you have a number?"

"Just call the station."

The two of them left.

"Don't ye want tae check the room?" asked Broch as he jogged to keep up with her.

"No. I don't want to know anything about the DNA left in

that place."

"DNA?"

She dismissed his confusion with a wave. "Some other time."

He still had a lot of questions.

"Ye called yerself *Cathy Jones*."

"I lied."

"Dae ye hae a family name?"

Catriona glanced at him.

"Yes. *Phoenix*. No relation."

He scowled. "Nae relation tae whit?"

"Oh, sorry. If you live in Hollywood and your last name is Phoenix—people tend to confuse you with another family."

He said the name in his head a few times and found he liked the ring of it. "*Catriona Phoenix*. It's a nice name."

"Thank you. I picked it myself when I was little."

"Wherefer dae we go noo? Dae ye ken where Sean is?"

"Yes. No. *Maybe*." She huffed as she dropped into the seat of her car. "*Wherefer* we go now is home to pack, do a few Internet searches, and then we're going to fly to Tennessee."

Broch stared back at the motel as she started the Jeep and pulled out of the parking lot. They were on the road for five minutes when something Catriona had said rang in his head like a broken bell.

"Hold now. Did ye say *fly*?"

CHAPTER TWENTY-ONE

They entered the payroll office, and Jeanie beamed.

"Hello."

"Hello, darlin'," said Broch. Catriona turned in time to see him wink at the receptionist.

Jeanie giggled.

Catriona groaned and opened the elevator. "Jeanie, see if you can track down Lulu. She's probably in her trailer. Tell her I'm coming to see her in about twenty minutes, and it's important."

Jeanie's eyebrows tilted like opening saloon doors. "Lulu? Really? She scares me."

"Don't let her bully you. If she says she's busy or complains in any way, tell her *tattoo,* and that'll shut her up."

Jeanie saluted. "Will do."

Catriona found Broch peering intently at a fantasy movie poster hanging on the wall behind Jeanie's desk and grabbed his wrist to pull him onto the elevator.

"Are those real?" he asked.

She glanced at the poster. On it, flying dragons terrorized New York City.

She nodded.

"Yep. A dragon crashed into the Statue of Liberty about a year ago." She pointed to the statute on the poster so he'd know what she meant.

He gaped. "Dragons are real? Dae they live near here?"

She shrugged. "New Zealand, mostly."

He pressed his lower lip against his top and nodded, inadvertently doing what Catriona considered a passable Robert DeNiro impression.

"Huh," he grunted.

They stepped off the elevator, and Catriona strode down the hall to open the door to Broch's apartment. "Get anything you need for the trip and meet me back at my place."

"Where are we going again?"

"Tennessee."

She heard him call, "Whit's Tennessee?" as she entered her apartment but decided they'd have plenty of time to talk about it during the trip.

Opening her laptop, Catriona searched for Thorn Campbell, combined with *Tennessee*. His name popped up in the *LaFollette Press* about a drug bust a few years earlier. The paper served the Campbell County area of the state.

"You've got to be kidding me. He could be living amongst his descendants," she mumbled aloud. She tried to narrow down the location of his home but found no more information.

She felt confident Thorn didn't have access to a private plane. If he was headed to Tennessee, he was driving.

That gave them time to get there first.

Three loud knocks on the door made her jump, and she jogged to open it. In the hall, Broch stood holding a plastic dry-cleaning bag.

"Whit's this?" he demanded to know.

She eyed the bag. His kilt hung neatly folded and pinned to a hanger inside.

"Your dry cleaning?"

He stormed past her into the apartment and tossed the bag on the sofa before tearing it. Holding the contents aloft, he asked again.

"Whit's *this*?"

"Your skirt."

"Mah—" He squinted at her, his lips twisted into a knot.

"You're daein' that on purpose noo."

She smirked. It was true.

"Feel it," he said, shoving the kilt toward her.

She reached out and touched it. "Soft."

"*Exactly*. Dae ye ken the time it took me tae get this kilt to the right texture? T'was damn near *weatherproof*."

"You mean from all the skin oil and dirt on it?"

"*Aye*."

Her lip curled. "Ew."

He released a breath as his arms flopped to his sides like a deflating balloon. "This is *terrible*."

"I'm sure Jeanie was trying to do you a favor. Do you have everything you need?" She returned to her Internet search.

His shoulders dropped another half inch. "Howfur am ah to pack when ah dinnae even ken where ah'm going? Ah'm I needing a weapon? How much food and water should ah bring?"

She sighed. "I forget sometimes who I'm talking to." She swiveled on her stool to face him. "I meant to pack a change of clothes and toothpaste. We're not marching through Middle Earth with a band of Hobbits—"

"Ooh." His eyes lit. "Toothpaste? The fine minty sauce in the tiny, crinkly sack? Ah like that. But I ate it all. Dae ye hae another?"

She looked up from her keyboard. "Minty sauce?" Her hand rose to cover her mouth. "You *ate* the toothpaste?"

He nodded.

She took a deep breath and expelled it with a pop. "Okay. No worries. I'll bring more."

He clapped his hands together. "Ooh. Kin ah bring the soap tae?"

"Please tell me you didn't eat the soap."

He scowled. "How come would ah eat that? It tastes *terrible*—"

"How do you know what it tastes—"

"—ah lik' the way it makes me feel, though." He rubbed his hands up and down his body as if mimicking a shower.

She shut the laptop. "I'm going to get a shower and pack. Go grab your soap—go crazy and grab the shampoo, too—and we'll get out of here."

He nodded and strode away. Catriona took her shower. By the time she returned to her living room, bag in hand, Broch had reappeared, holding a familiar white plastic bag. She caught a whiff of air freshener.

She pointed at it.

"*No. Dude.* You can't use a scented trash bag for luggage. Dump your stuff in here." Sitting her bag on the back of the sofa, she zipped it open.

"But mine smells *fine*," he whined.

"Absolutely not."

Scowling, Broch dumped the contents of the scented trash bag into her carry-on. A wet bar of soap, a bottle of shampoo, and a ceramic surfboard tumbled on top of her neatly folded clothing. It wasn't until she noticed all the white specks spilling onto her clothes that she realized the surfboard was a salt shaker.

She looked at him.

"You're sure that's it? You don't want to bring a lamp or the sofa—"

"Can ah bring the glowing time?"

It took her a moment to divine what he meant. "You mean the alarm clock? *No.* They'll have those where we're going."

He rolled his lips in, seemed to think for a moment, and then handed his kilt to her.

"Put this in there, tae. Even though it's *ruined*."

She shook her head. "We're not going to be in a situation where you can wear this."

He pointed to the bag, looking as determined as a headstrong child.

"Where ah gae, it gaes."

With a sigh, she pressed the kilt into the bag, zipped it closed and pushed her high-sodium luggage out of her mind.

"Let's go."

Catriona took a few steps toward the door and then stopped.

Oh no.

She set her bag on the ground and leaned against the wall.

Her right hand rose to her chest.

Broch took a step toward her. She held her other hand aloft to ward him off and slid down the wall to sit on her heels. Taking deep, slow breaths, she cleared her mind.

No matter how much air she sucked in, it felt as though no oxygen reached her lungs.

She tried not to panic.

Broch squatted beside her.

"Darlin', yer scarin' me. Whit can ah dae fur ye?"

"It's a panic attack. It'll pass," she whispered.

"Panic?"

"Anxiety. Too much. It makes my heart race...hard to breathe."

She shuddered, her body shaking as if she'd been left in the cold for hours.

"Och. Come here." His lips pressed into a hard line, and he nodded once, like a man who'd decided it was time to take control of the situation.

He sat on the floor in front of her and spread his legs. Grabbing her feet, he spread her legs as well, lifting them over his own until one sat on either side of his hips. Scooting forward, he slipped his hand around her back and pulled her against his chest.

The shock of the sudden movement almost made Catriona forget her attack. At first, she resisted, fearing his bear hug would smother the last of the breath from her lungs, but as her legs wrapped around his waist and her body pressed against his, she found unexpected comfort in the slow rhythm of his chest rising and falling against her own.

Her shaking slowed as her breathing matched his.

"In and out," he spoke softly in her ear. "There ye go, deary. In and out."

They sat like that, breathing as one for several minutes until nausea subsided, and she felt she could breathe normally again. Still, she clung to him long after the attack had passed.

She couldn't remember the last time she'd been held.

He nuzzled beneath her ear. Her lips parted, and she nearly kissed his neck before realizing *his* nuzzling hadn't been romantic but rather the result of him shifting his hips.

His legs are falling asleep.

She pulled back, and he let her slide from his embrace.

"Thank you. That helped." Embarrassed, she avoided his eyes. She tried to stand, but he reached out and put a hand on her thigh.

"Lassie—my mother Blair was proud and brave as a lion, but ah more than once found her sobbing in the stables such as ah thought she would die fae lack o' air. She hid her fears and worries 'til such a time she could release them, lik' the river after a storm. Ah think ye dae the same. Tis nothin' tae be ashamed aboot."

Catriona felt her eyes well with tears.

His gaze softened another notch.

"Ah know. Come here."

He snatched her back into his arms and squeezed her, swaying her back and forth in an exaggerated manner until she began to laugh.

"Okay, okay," she said, slapping his shoulder. "I'm fine now. I'm good."

"Dae ye feel better? Ah'll swing the fear and sadness oot of ye. Here we gae—"

He rocked harder, bouncing from one butt cheek to the other until she pushed away from him, laughing and crying at the same time.

"You're *insane*," she said, standing and wiping her tears.

"Next time you're feeling heavy, ye hug me or batter me or pound on mah chest 'til yer feelin' better, aye?"

"Yes, fine, fine. Get up, you goon."

He jumped to his feet and touched his hair with both hands. "But ye cannae muss mah locks fur ah hae it just *sae*."

Her eyes drew to his head, and she reached to touch his hair. It was *stiff*.

"You found the hair spray," she said.

He nodded sadly. "Tis all gone noo."

"I can feel that."

"We need mair."

"I'll get *mair* when we get back."

"Good. Let's go then, ye big baby."

She gasped, and he laughed a deep belly laugh as she pretended to swing at him.

Gathering up their things, they left the apartment.

Catriona couldn't stop smiling.

It was so *weird.*

Downstairs, she grabbed a piece of paper Jeanie held out to her as they passed. As she opened the front door, she heard Broch behind her.

"Ah need to talk to ye later, Miss Jeanie, aboot mah *kilt.*"

Outside, Broch headed for the car, but Catriona walked past it to a golf cart. She got in and pulled it to where he stood.

"We're taking the wee one?" he asked.

"Yep."

He shrugged and sat beside her, studying the pedal and steering wheel as she drove off.

"Ye hae sae many ways tae travel noo, but ah haven't seen *one* horse. Whit hae ye done with them?"

She sniffed. "The dragons. Horses are their favorite food, you know."

Catriona glanced at Broch to see his mouth hanging open.

His expression made everything up until that moment *worth it.*

Catriona parked the golf cart next to a trailer, hopped out, and knocked on the door. An older woman in a bright pink turban speckled with fake diamonds answered.

"This had better be good," she said, lighting a cigarette.

"Lulu, you know you're not supposed to smoke in the

trailers," said Catriona.

The woman rolled her black-rimmed eyes. "Oh *please*."

"May we come in?"

Lulu peered over Catriona's shoulder to ogle Broch.

"Oh *my*. You brought me a present."

Lulu stepped aside to allow them entry.

Catriona held the door open as Broch passed her to enter the trailer. He paused as if hoping for a moment to confer before walking into the dragon's den, but Lulu grabbed the waist of his jeans and jerked him inside.

CHAPTER TWENTY-TWO

"Sit *here*, handsome," said Lulu, shooing a long-legged white standard poodle from the trailer's velvet loveseat. The poodle gave her a look that would have killed a cat and flopped on the ground a few feet away.

Lulu pushed Catriona toward a stand-alone chair and guided Broch to the loveseat before melting into the cushion beside him. The claw not holding her cigarette slid down his chest and perched on the shelf of his pectoral muscle.

"Tell me what you need," she purred.

Catriona sat in her chair. "Easy, Lu. Your charms are lost on him. He's not trying to catch a break in Hollywood, and he has no idea who you are."

Lulu recoiled to gape at Broch. "You don't know who I am? How is that possible? I'm famous in the farthest reaches of all seven continents."

Catriona paused, considering her options.

If she told the aging movie queen that Broch was from some faraway destination, she'd have to sit and wait while Lulu named all her movies, searching for some glimmer of recognition in Broch's eye. Even if they insisted he'd been living in a monastery since birth, Lulu's ego wouldn't let it go.

Then she remembered Lulu didn't listen to a word that wasn't about *her*.

Why not tell the truth?

"He's from eighteenth-century Scotland."

Lulu paused before releasing a loud, opened-mouthed laugh. Her square, white dentures flashed like a row of painted bricks. Clinging to the side of Broch's chest like a koala baby, she stared up into his face. "I wish that was true. You could be my big, handsome Highlander."

Catriona grinned. As expected, Lulu only heard the part she wanted to hear. *Sexy young Highlander.*

Lulu pet his cheek. "I'll get you copies of my films. Maybe we can watch them *together*."

Broch's eyes flashed with fear, and Catriona placed her finger over her lips to pantomime a request for silence. He offered Lulu an uncomfortable smile.

"Sounds fine," he said.

Lulu cackled with delight.

Though watching Broch squirm beneath Lulu's affection amused her to no end, Catriona decided it was time to get back to business.

"So, Lu, before you unhook your jaw and swallow poor Broch here whole—"

"I've been known to do that," said Lulu, her eyes never leaving Broch's. "If you know what I mean."

A bead of sweat appeared on his brow.

Catriona barreled on. "—I need to ask you a favor."

"Of course. Anything for you, Cat dear." Lulu traced the sharp edge of Brock's jaw with her crimson-painted fingernail.

"I need your plane," said Catriona.

The request caught Lulu's attention, and she leaned away from Broch to better peer at Catriona.

"My plane? Why?"

"Sean's in trouble. I can't get into details, but I have to get to Tennessee faster than someone can drive."

"Well, sweetie, that's why God made *Southwest Airlines*—for people like you."

Catriona shook her head. "Can't. Broch doesn't have identification. I need your *special* plane. The one that doesn't ask questions about the pretty boys you import from South

America."

Lulu grinned as if remembering something pleasant and then pointed at Broch with a crooked claw. "He's illegal?"

"As illegal as they come."

"Really?"

If it were possible, Lulu seemed even more enraptured with the Highlander. She ran the hand holding her cigarette through Broch's dark hair. Catriona winced, fearing the ember might set his hair spray experiment aflame.

"Lu, please. It's important."

"Is he a terrorist? I can't give my plane to just *anyone*."

Catriona widened her eyes at Broch, silently begging him to help their cause.

He cleared his throat. "Aye, Lulu, ye hae me dead tae rights. Ah *ah'm* a terrorist."

Catriona dropped her head into her hands.

Oh no, no, no.

"You are?" asked Lulu, withdrawing.

Broch stopped her hand from pulling away from his chest and leered, his voice dropping to a soft, husky tone. "Aye. *I'll terrorize your loins.*"

Catriona's jaw dropped.

Wait. What?

Lulu giggled like a schoolgirl and tweaked his nipple through his t-shirt. Broch jumped and attempted a laugh, though it sounded more like a suppressed squeal of pain.

Lulu leaned back and raised her cigarette to her lips. The ash, which had grown over an inch long, fell into her lap. She ignored it as Catriona fought the urge to slap at it.

"Fine. I'll trade you the plane for a weekend with—"

Lulu held up her hand, creating a wall between herself and Broch, and then used her other hand to surreptitiously point at him from behind it.

"*Him,*" she whispered.

Catriona shook her head. "He isn't mine to bargain with. He isn't trying to climb the ladder."

Lulu tittered. "I've been called a lot of things but never a *ladder."*

Catriona smiled. "Sorry. Can't do it."

Lulu pouted. "Hm. Okay. How about this? You can have the plane, but you have to take the girls. They have a hairdressing appointment in New York in three days anyway. You'll save me the trip."

"Why New York? Can't they get groomed here?"

Lulu's brow crinkled. "Are you mad? This place is crawling with *hacks.*"

Catriona sighed. "Fine. I don't mind taking them, but we're going to *Tennessee,* not New York."

Lulu dismissed her concerns with a wave of her hand and sent another chunk of ash fluttering to the ground. "I'll have a car pick them up and take them the rest of the way."

"*Thank you.* But we have to go *now.*"

"Fine. I'll call and have them prepare the plane. Do you have a preference for a flight crew? Girls? Boys? Open to interpretation?"

"Any regular old flight crew is fine. We're going to help Sean, not explore our sexual boundaries."

Lulu nodded. "Excellent. That will save me a fortune. I'll have the girls out in a moment." The diva stood, took Broch's face in her palm, and kissed him square on the mouth. She winked at Catriona and swept past the poodle to enter a closed door at the back of the trailer, dog tight on her heels.

Catriona stood and nodded toward the front door. Broch jumped to his feet and followed her out, nearly knocking her over in his haste.

"Wha wis that? She's git a tongue lik' an eel."

Catriona giggled. "She's a famous actress. Been with the studio for nearly fifty years. I think she liked you."

The Highlander grunted.

"I'm nae sure that's good," he said, wiping ruby lipstick from his lips with the back of his hand.

Catriona patted his arm. "No, it's good. You don't want to be on the *wrong* side of her attention, believe me."

Still smacking his lips as if to rid them of a foul taste, Broch glared.

"Ye used me lik' a piece o' beef. Ye could hae *warned* me."

"Sorry. I should have. I'm well aware it never hurts to bring a good-looking young man to a Lulu meeting."

Broch's scowl shifted to a smirk.

"Sae, ye think ah'm good-lookin'?"

She shrugged. "Eh."

He chuckled and glanced back at the trailer. "Her girls...ye ken, ah dinnae think tis safe tae take her daughters tae war with us."

"They won't be near the action, and they're not—"

The door to the trailer flung open, and two white standard poodles ran down the stairs. Lulu trailed behind at the opposite end of their pink rhinestone-studded leashes. It was impossible to tell which dog was the one they'd seen displaced from its spot on the loveseat. The two were identical.

Lulu slapped the leashes into Broch's hand. "Here. They'll have the plane ready when you get there."

He looked down at the poodles.

"These are yer lassies?"

"These are my *poodles*. Lassie was a collie. I knew it. Dumb as a box of rocks." Lulu put her face close to Broch's. "I want you to know, you sexy hunk of haggis, if you *ever* feel the urge, feel free to come back and see me sometime."

Broch nodded. "Aye. Thank you...?"

Lulu tapped his cheek twice and, with a sweep of her silk kimono, re-entered the trailer, slamming the door behind her.

CHAPTER TWENTY-THREE

When the rocking stopped, Sean awoke to find himself still in the trunk of Thorn's car. He'd willed himself to sleep for what he hoped had been a few hours. The way they'd tied his arms and legs, his discomfort was nearly unbearable. Worse, it reminded him he wasn't young anymore.

It took him a moment to realize he'd been awakened by the sound of Thorn berating one of his henchmen.

"You gave your license to the guy at the hotel?" screamed the voice he recognized as Thorn's. It sounded as if he were standing outside the car.

"Yes. I mean, he *asked* for it," said another, meeker man.

"You moron. Don't you understand? If they pull records at that motel, it could lead them *right to you*. Right to your damn *house*."

"Who's going to find it? Who's looking for us in Tennessee? That girl and the dude in the skirt?"

Sean heard a *crack!* and suspected Thorn had smacked the other man.

"It's not a *skirt*, you jackass. It's a kilt. And we left a dead man a few hundred yards from that hotel. Get it? *Somebody will check the hotel.*" Thorn roared with frustration. "Get in the damn car."

Car doors opened and closed, and the vehicle shook. The engine started. Sean felt them ease back onto the road.

He licked his lips. They hadn't thought to offer him water and his throat felt parched. There *were* gaps between the trunk and the main compartment of the car that allowed air conditioning to trickle through, but the trunk remained hot.

But, he'd learned something. He knew Thorn left behind a thread. That gave him both hope and additional concerns.

When Luther grabbed his phone, did he call the police or Catriona?

His attempts to distract Thorn's gang from Luther, as his friend crawled across his kitchen floor, had gotten him clobbered. Only the throbbing in his limbs distracted him from the ache in his head.

He knew from overheard conversations they were headed to Tennessee and did the math in his head. It would take them thirty-two hours on the road, more or less, to make the trip. It seemed they wouldn't be stopping to sleep.

No way to tell how long it would take Catriona to put the pieces of his abduction together. And did he even want Catriona to find him? Better she stays safe in California.

Broch would watch over her. He could take over as Catriona's guardian. If only he'd had time to explain everything to the boy.

Sean always knew he'd have to leave. He just hadn't thought the end would come at the hands of the man who killed his wife.

That part bothered him to no end.

CHAPTER TWENTY-FOUR

"Ah dinnae lik' this," said Broch as Catriona buckled his seat belt.

He'd felt ill since first laying eyes on the airplane.

Flying wasn't *natural*.

Catriona patted his hand and sat in the seat beside him. "I'll be right here beside you. It's the least I can do, after what you did for me." She wiped a smudge of Lulu's red lipstick from his cheek with her thumb, and he looked away, embarrassed.

He stared through the round window. "Ah see it haes wings, but ah dinnae see howfur they can *flap*."

Catriona laughed. "They don't *flap*. There's an engine in it, like cars. They, um—it has something to do with the air moving over the wings and lift and—" She waved a hand at him. "It doesn't matter. We'll be fine. Take my word for it."

He sighed. "Aye. That's reassuring. Ah feel much better noo, Professor."

The engines roared to life and Broch grabbed Catriona's hand. She put her other hand on top of his and held it tight.

"Seriously. You'll be fine. I promise."

He believed her. *Mostly*.

He put his other hand on top of the pile.

"Ah'll hold on tae ye fer a bit."

He did his best to feign bravery, but by the time they were in the air, he felt sure the frozen meat pie he'd found in the giant silver box back at the apartment would be as *easy* coming back up as it had been *difficult* going down.

There was no place in that 'apartment' to start a proper fire.

The young woman who'd ushered them onto the plane appeared from behind a curtain.

"Can I get either of you something to drink? Or maybe—"

"Aye, a whiskey," said Broch before she'd finished her sentence.

"Certainly. And you, miss?"

Catriona tugged her hand from Broch's grasp. He hadn't realized he was still holding it.

"Bottle of water, please."

When the woman left, Catriona leaned toward him. "You should try and drink water. Flights dry you out."

He scoffed, searching for signs of the plane lady and his whiskey. "Ah intend tae dry oot the plane."

"Still not feeling safe?"

"Na. I'm fine." The hum of the engines unnerved him, but he guessed it was better to hear them than to *not*.

She patted his arm. "Good. If you don't mind, I'm going to lie down for a bit. I didn't get enough sleep last night."

"Howfur long until we're in Tennessee?"

"Between four and five hours, I think."

He sighed.

Catriona stood and moved to a bed at the back of the plane. He peered back at her over the seats, wishing he could be calm enough to lie down.

The plane lady returned and handed him a half-filled glass and a tiny bottle of light brown liquid.

The glass smelled like whiskey, but the tiny bottle amused him to no end.

"Whit's this?"

"Your whiskey, sir. I poured you one and brought you another, so you'll have it handy."

"Did ye steal it fae a faerie?"

"I'm sorry?"

"Ah dinnae want tae anger the wee folk by swallyin' all

their whiskey."

She laughed. "I think you're safe."

He sighed. "That's wit everybody keeps tellin' me."

He drank his glass in a single gulp and stared out the window at the clouds passing before cracking and pouring the tiny bottle. Beneath him, the plane rumbled steadily, and he decided it might be wise to sleep. It would keep his mind off moving with the birds in a giant metal contraption that had no right being off the ground.

He stood to make his way back to the bed across from Catriona's, only to find the twin poodles stretched on it.

"Ye'll need tae shift, dogs," he whispered, motioning for them to move.

Each dog opened a single eye and stared at him. They seemed unimpressed by his command.

"Come. Git, *noo*."

One of the dogs stretched her long legs, taking up what little space remained. The other lifted her poofy white head, which Broch took as a good sign.

"There ye go, lassie. Hop off."

She yawned, and her head flopped back down.

Broch placed a hand on one dog's rump, meaning to lift her. She growled. He retracted his hand and glanced at Catriona. While he thought he'd win a wrestling match with the fuzzy white demons, the commotion was sure to wake Catriona, who appeared blissful in her nap.

He sighed and returned to his seat.

Closing his eyes, he recalled holding Catriona during her panic attack. The memory of his mother Blair had come to him upon seeing Catriona there, sitting on the ground, back against the wall. He hadn't found it odd. Glimpses of his life before his time travel had been popping into his mind ever since he awoke on the studio lot. A bit of fabric reminded him of Mother Rose's dress, running water made him recall playing by the river, and a patch of blue sky brought memories of tending to the garden on the side of his mothers' cottage.

He never knew when or what might return to him.

Many of the images didn't fit his life with the Broken Women. Upon seeing cars, he'd had a flash of a similar vehicle, but couldn't place it.

Did ah travel through time before?

The plane shook as if it had hit a bump in the road, and he grabbed the arms of his seat, the bandage on his wound pulling. He winced and put his hand to it, only to suffer another flash of déjà vu. The cabin of the plane disappeared. Instead, he saw the house where he'd grown up as if he were standing a hundred feet from it.

Something made him look down.

Blood pooled at his feet.

Not my blood.

He knew whose blood it was.

Blair's.

The pool ran from the body of Mother Blair. Mighty Blair, her neck nearly severed, her eyes open and staring, lay on the ground beside him.

A sputtering noise caught his attention, and a few feet away, he saw a dying man dressed in black leather armor. He recognized the sword in the man's belly as his own.

Stumbling toward the house, he found Mother Rose, dead, curled in a heap at the entrance, most of the clothes torn from her body. Inside, Mother Margaret and another old woman, who'd only recently come to stay with them, lay dead as well.

He cried out and fell to his knees, pulling Mother Margaret's lifeless body into his lap. He rocked her, demanding that she awaken, until, through his tear-filled eyes, he caught a glimpse of his own bloodstained hands.

The hands of a boy.

Gently, he eased Mother Margaret's body back to the ground. Scrambling to his feet, he ran back outside. The dying man was dead. He realized now how small the sword in the man's belly was. Blair had the sword made especially for him—a weapon small enough for a boy's hand.

"Even the tail of a wasp does its damage," she'd said upon presenting it to him.

He jogged to the water trough and stared at his reflection in the dark water.

A child, no older than twelve, stared back at him.

"No."

He fell back, gaze drifting across the field.

Men.

Four men on horseback traveled away from the house. The armor they wore resembled that of the dead man beside Blair. This man had stayed behind, perhaps to have his way with Blair, and found it would be easier to kill her than steal her honor.

That's when Broch arrived.

He remembered. Blair had seen him seconds before the man slit her throat. She'd grabbed the bastard's head to keep him from turning. She might have kept fighting, but instead, she'd distracted their common enemy to keep him from harm.

Broch stabbed the man as he fell back, exhausted from his battle with Mother Blair.

"Come back!" Broch yelled at the four retreating horsemen.

I'll kill you all!

The lead man held up a hand, and they reined in their horses. They turned.

The leader's arm raised again, this time to point at Broch.

He sees me.

The man began to gallop toward him.

He's coming.

That's when Broch realized the importance of the man's reaction. There was no reason to ride back to kill a boy unless—

He was here for me.

He killed everyone looking for me.

"Broch?"

Broch jumped and grabbed the wrist of the hand touching his shoulder.

"Ow!"

It took a moment for his vision to clear. Catriona stood beside him, her wrist tucked firmly in his grasp.

Embarrassed, he released her.

"Sorry. Ah was dreamin'."

"Bad dream? You were moaning."

Broch nodded. "Aye. Ah wish it so."

"We're about there."

He nodded and noticed a new tiny bottle of whiskey on the tray beside him.

He cracked it open and drank it down.

CHAPTER TWENTY-FIVE

The poodle twins led the way from the plane, followed by Catriona at the end of their leashes. Broch hauled their overnight bag on his shoulder.

A man rolled up in a John Deere Gator, a vehicle that looked as if a dune buggy and a lawnmower had had a baby. He wore a flannel shirt with rolled sleeves and a wide grin.

"Hey, y'all. I'm Rusty, and I'm here to give you a lift. Hop on in."

Catriona took her seat beside the man. Broch sat in the back with a poodle secured beneath each arm.

Rusty shuttled them to a dark brown building not far from the runway.

When they rolled to a stop, Broch hopped off the back and danced out of the way to avoid tangling in the dogs' leashes. The poodles paced around him, attempting to smell everything in sight.

"You need a ride into town?" Rusty asked, reaching for Catriona's bag.

She shook her head. "There should be a car here to drop us off at a hotel."

Rusty led them inside and took his place behind a desk.

"You mean the car for the poodles?" he asked as if he'd been thinking about her response the entire trip to the door.

"Yes. Is it here?"

He shook his head. "Nope. Not coming."

Catriona gaped. "*What*?"

"Got a call while you were in the air. The car isn't coming."

"Why?"

"She didn't say. To be honest, she was kinda, uh…"

"Abrupt?"

"Yeah. Sure. That works."

"*Lulu*," Catriona growled. She tilted back her head and stared at the ceiling, trying to formulate a plan.

"I guess we can put them on the plane and send them back to her…" she mused aloud.

Rusty shook his head again.

She scowled. "No?"

"Nope. The plane is already on its way to Argentina."

Catriona strode to the window in time to see the plane taking off.

"*No—*"

She clenched her fists.

Lulu. Broch must have reminded the old horndog of her polo players, and she'd dialed up a delivery.

Catriona turned back to the man behind the desk.

"Did Lulu share any thoughts on what I'm supposed to do with these dogs?"

"Yup. The car will be here in three days."

"*Three days?* I can't wait here three days."

Rusty shrugged.

Catriona hung her head. "This is a disaster."

"Looks lik' we'll be spending time together, lassies," said Broch to the dogs.

"Of course, it wouldn't even occur to Lulu this might be an inconvenience for *me*," groaned Catriona.

She moved back to the desk.

"Is there some sort of doggie hotel in town?" she asked.

Rusty coughed a laugh and wiped his nose with the back of his hand. "Have you seen this town?"

"I'll take that for a *no*. Do you live near here?"

He nodded.

"How'd you like to make a hundred bucks watching these two highly intelligent, clean, polite dogs for a couple of days?"

He shook his head. "Nope."

"Two hundred?"

"It's not about the money. I'm a cat person."

She dropped her chin to stare at him from beneath her brow. "*You're a cat person.*"

He nodded. "Princess Paw and her court would have a ten alarm meltdown if I brought those slobbering Q-tips home."

Catriona couldn't believe her luck. If this was how the rest of their rescue mission was going to go, they'd be better off packing up and heading home now.

She shook her head. "So, we're here with the only cat man in Tennessee."

Rusty laughed. "Well, now, that's not even close to true. I belong to a group called the Cat-Men-Do, and you couldn't find a bigger group of cat lovers."

Catriona gave him a minute to admit he was pulling her leg, but his expression remained sincere.

"Okaaay... Well, I guess I'd like to take you up on that lift to town after all if that's okay?"

"No problem. Yours was the last flight of the day. I can take you on my way home."

"We'd appreciate that."

"Whit are we doing?" asked Broch as the dogs pulled him past her.

"We're going to town to find a hotel that takes dogs and someone who knows where we can find Thorn—"

"Thorn?" said Rusty as he put on his jacket. "Thorn *Campbell*?"

Broch pulled the dogs short, and both he and Catriona's attention turned to Rusty.

"Yes. You know him?" asked Catriona, wondering how she could have been so stupid as to say Thorn's name out loud in what was probably his hometown.

Rusty nodded. "Thorn? Sure. Everybody around here knows him."

"You know where he lives?"

"Yup."

A silence fell as he shut down the electronics and lights. Finished, he took a place by the door. "Ready?"

"Not quite," said Catriona. "I was hoping you could *share* that information with us."

"What?"

"Where Thorn lives."

"Oh. Well, yes and no. For one, no one knows where he lives *exactly*. His place don't have a postal address, if you know what I mean."

"He doesn't live in a house?"

"No, I mean…" Rusty scratched at his head. "You know, I never thought about it. I *reckon* he lives in a house, it's just *out there*." He pointed out the back door through which they'd entered.

"You mean out in the woods somewhere?"

"Yes, but also, I mean *literally* out *there*. Cut across the airport until you see a patch of woods. Work your way through those trees for a couple of miles, and you'll come across a holler. Cross that holler, and he's somewhere up on the hill on the other side."

Catriona stared through the window at the woods. "I assume he doesn't tramp through the *holler* every time he wants to buy eggs? Surely there's a road?"

"Nope."

Rusty motioned for them to follow him out the front door.

"How does he come and go?" asked Catriona as Rusty locked the door behind them.

"He's got himself a helicopter and an army of ATVs. That's why everyone knows *basically* where he lives, but not *exactly*. We see the helicopter." Staring at the woods, he paused to suck his tooth with his tongue. "He's a drug dealer, you know."

Catriona's eyes widened. "Is it safe for you to tell me that?"

Rusty shrugged. "Not like it's a secret."

"What if we were cops?"

Rusty snorted a laugh. "Cops aren't usually a pretty girl, a pretty boy, and a pair of foofy dogs."

"It's the hair spray," said Broch, gingerly touching his hair. He looked at Catriona. "Ah tellt ye."

She heard Broch but didn't have time to compliment his grooming.

"We need to get going."

"My truck's over here," said Rusty, walking toward a black Ford pickup truck parked in the airport's lot.

She held up a hand.

"Nevermind. Thank you, but we won't need the ride after all."

Rusty's head cocked. "What's that?"

"We don't need the ride. I appreciate it, though."

Rusty put his hands in his pockets and surveyed the area, so she was sure to notice his point.

"There ain't nobody else around here. The next human being you'll see is me tomorrow morning. You're not going to get a taxi out here."

Catriona nodded. "I know. We're fine."

Rusty shrugged and waved as he walked to his truck. "Suit yerselves."

As he drove away, Catriona turned to Broch.

"We're aff tae cross the field and head intae the woods, aren't we?" he asked before she had a chance to break the news.

She nodded.

"Yep."

CHAPTER TWENTY-SIX

They crossed the airfield and hefted the poodles over the fence to the opposite side. The procedure required Broch to climb half the fence with a poodle under his arm while Catriona sat balanced at the top. He handed her the sixty-pound dog, and she cradled it while he shimmied to the other side. Then she handed the dog to him, and he lowered it to the ground before returning to get its furry counterpart.

He hefted the second dog to her.

"I'm going to *kill* Lulu for this," Catriona grunted, poodle squirming in her arms.

Once everyone reached the other side, Broch released the dogs from their leashes. They looked at him, looked at each other, and then tore into the forest.

"What are you doing?" asked Catriona, horrified.

Broch wrapped up the leashes. "They're dogs. They should be runnin' aroond."

"Those dogs have spent their lives sleeping on beds and being spoon-fed beef tartar. They don't know how to survive out here. If anything happens to them…"

He waved a hand at her. "Eh. They'll be fine."

Catriona scowled and tromped through the underbrush in the direction Rusty had pointed—what she hoped was the most direct route to Sean. Or, hopefully, the place Thorn *would* be bringing Sean. She hoped they'd get there first and have time to set a trap.

Broch watched the sun and kept them on target. Every few minutes, the dogs ripped by them before vanishing again. After fifteen minutes of play, they fell into line beside their human companions, happily panting, tongues lolling.

"See? Ah tellt ye." Broch said, motioning to their new white shadows.

"Hm. And it's *told*. Not *tellt*."

"Who tellt ye that? Ah was tellt different."

She chuckled. "Funny."

After an hour of struggling over rough terrain, the forest gave way. Broch and Catriona found themselves staring into a shallow valley, illuminated by a nearly full moon. On the opposite side of the notch sat a house atop the ridge, a single light glowing in its window.

"That must be Thorn's place," said Catriona.

"It's a good spot. Hard tae creep up on them perched on the hill lik' that."

"I guess we'll cross through the…what did Rusty call it? The holler?"

Broch rubbed his chin, his gaze dancing across the landscape. He dropped the bag from his shoulder, unzipped it, and pulled his kilt from inside. Flipping it out, he laid it on the flattest available area. No sooner did he drop it than both dogs flopped on top.

"Are we having a picnic?" asked Catriona.

"We'll go na closer tonight."

"Why?"

"Fer one, ye tellt me he wouldn't be there until tomorrow at the earliest."

"Yes, but—"

"Fer two, ah need tae *think*."

He pulled bottle after bottle of water from the bag and lined them up like soldiers at the edge of the kilt. Cupping his hands, he nodded to the bottles.

"Fer the dogs."

She cracked one open and poured it into his makeshift

palm bowl. The dogs took turns drinking.

"I was wondering why that bag felt so heavy. Did you take every bottle of water on the plane?"

"Aye. All the whiskey and some of these bags that smell good."

He tossed a bag of peanuts at her.

When the dogs had their fill of water, she cracked a bottle for herself and handed one to Broch. He ignored it and instead handed her a tiny whiskey.

She eyed the little bottle. "I'll drink one of these if you hydrate. You're like a camel."

She thrust the bottle of water at him again.

Broch took it and drank it down. Next, he opened a few packets of peanuts and fed them to the dogs while they sipped whiskey and stared at Thorn's hideout.

"Are you sure we shouldn't keep going?" asked Catriona. "Maybe it would be *good* to travel under cover of darkness?"

He shook his head. "Lassie, ah ken nothing aboot this land, and they *live* here. They'll see us coming afore we can lay eyes on them. Ah'm here tae help, nae tae watch ye run tae yer death."

She sighed. "If you say so. You're the outdoorsy guy, I guess."

"Aye. At light, ah'll creep about and see what we're up against."

She nodded as a shiver ran through her. "I didn't realize how chilly it would be."

"We should get some sleep. We can squeeze between these two furballs and work up some warmth."

He pushed his way between the poodles and motioned to her to join him.

Catriona stared down at the man, her arms wrapped around her chest. It seemed odd to lie beside him. She still didn't know him well, but he hadn't done *anything* to betray her trust. Quite the contrary. He'd helped her with Jaxson, been kind during her panic attack, and he'd come with her to Tennessee to save Sean. He hadn't even complained about the two enormous—now filthy—standard poodles flanking him like columns on his freshly washed kilt blanket.

"Fine," she dropped to her knees and slid in beside him, pushing hard against the poodle to her left to make room. The poodle grunted her displeasure.

Tucked like a hot dog in a bun, with one arm against a poodle and one against Broch, Catriona sighed.

"I suppose this would be an elaborate stunt to get me alone in the woods. Especially since most of this was my idea."

He squinted one eye at her as if he didn't understand.

She attempted to clarify. "I mean, it feels a *little* like you're trying to set a romantic scene here."

He raised himself on his elbow. "Ye think this is *romantic*? Lyin' with dogs?"

She laughed. "Not that part..."

"Ye think ah'm going tae try tae kiss ye?"

"I..." She realized how conceited her comment had sounded. He hadn't made any real play for her affections.

He'd called her plain.

She'd forgotten about that.

She wasn't his type. Sure, he had a thing for being naked, but that had nothing to do with trying to impress her.

She sniffed, embarrassed. "Sorry. I'm only chattering. It's just that we're out here alone—"

He chuckled. "Lassie, if ah wanted tae kiss ye, ah'd just ask ye tae press yer lips on mine."

"And you're so certain I'd say yes?"

He nodded and made the face that reminded her of a rudimentary DeNiro impersonation.

"Aye."

"Oh? And why is that? Because you're so devastatingly handsome?"

"Na. Because ye want tae."

She raised on her elbow to look him in the eye. "Wait. You think I *want* to kiss you?"

"Aye."

"And who told you that?"

He shrugged. "Ye."

"Me? Funny, I don't remember saying that."

He grinned. "Yer eyes say it every time ye keek at me."

She barked a laugh. "And how exactly do I look at you?"

"Like this." He glanced away and then snapped back, his eyes a little wider, his gaze sweeping down her body and back again, clearly pantomiming a flirty leer.

She giggled. "You've got to be kidding. I do *not* look at you like that."

"You dae, but—"

"But what?"

"Yer scared of me."

"Scared? Why would I be scared?"

"I dinnae ken. Look at me, am lik' a wee puppy."

She chuckled, but behind the smile, her brain whirred, mulling his comment.

Am I scared of him?

He seemed so...*manly*. He was a different sort of creature from the men she usually met. More *raw*. More like the men she'd known as a child before Sean saved her.

Those men scared her.

She sighed. "I didn't mean to be rude—suggesting you were trying to get me alone. It's just, you know... You're from a time when men could do whatever they wanted with little consequence—"

Broch sat up. She could see by the look on his face she'd angered him. He thrust an index finger toward her, and her stomach tightened with nerves.

"Ye listen tae me, lassie. Ah would *never* take a wummin who didnae ask me tae be taken." His tone implied the disgust he held for the idea.

Catriona's face grew hot. "No, I didn't mean you—"

"There's na pleasure tae be had if the wummin takes na pleasure. Any man that would dae such a thing—"

She shook her hand, frantic to take back her comment. "I'm sorry. I was *projecting*. I had no reason—"

He huffed and flopped back down, crossing his burly arms

across his chest.

She bit her lip, waiting for him to talk.

He didn't.

She swallowed.

"Broch, I'm *sorry*. I really am. It was a terrible, insulting thing to say to you. You've been *nothing* but sweet to me. Nothing but a gentleman."

His lips, pressed tight, released. He looked away.

"I forgive ye," he said after a moment. "And ah apologize for saying ye were giving me the eye. Ah was only teasing ye."

"Thank you." She laid back down beside him and stared up at the stars.

I should probably just stop talking. Forever.

The uncomfortable silence between them grew.

"I'm glad we got that worked out," she said when the quiet became deafening.

Maybe a little talking.

He grunted.

"But I *wasn't* eyeing you. Let's be clear about that," she added.

"Of course nae."

She scowled.

Had she detected a hint of sarcasm?

"Right. I *wasn't*. We're clear on that."

"Aye. That's what ye said."

She hadn't imagined it.

He definitely sounded sarcastic.

She pulled up on her elbow and poked his pec with her index finger. The muscle was tight and springy like she remembered from the night she'd found him.

She felt her face grow warm with the memory.

Oh no...I felt him up when he was unconscious.

I'm the predator.

"Did ye just poke me?" he asked.

She snapped back to the present. "Huh? *Yes*. You're making it sound like you don't believe me."

He peered down his nose at her hand, drawing her

attention to it. She'd relaxed it, and her palm now rested on his chest.

She jerked it away.

"*Oh.* You think that was an excuse to touch you?"

He shrugged. "Ye said it. Nae me."

She huffed and rolled on her back.

"You're *infuriating*. You're lucky we only have one blanket, or I'd move."

"It's not a blanket," he muttered.

"Sorry, *kilt.* No. You know what? *Blanket.* I'll call it a *kilt* when you say *told* instead of *tellt* and *know* instead of *ken.* How do you like that?"

"I lik' it just fine."

"Fine."

"*Fine.*"

She scowled into the night sky. It made her *crazy* to think he thought she *wanted* him.

"We should sleep," he said.

She grunted in response and pulled the end of the bag they were using for a pillow beneath her neck. Somewhere nearby, an owl hooted. She'd never heard a real owl. If she hadn't been in her exact circumstances, she'd think it was someone playing a joke because *it sounded exactly like an owl.*

She traced the imaginary lines of the big dipper with her gaze and resisted the urge to continue the argument.

He thinks I want him. I know it, that infuriating son of a—

She nodded off until the poodle beside her began to snore, and her eyes popped open. She poked the dog beside her, and she placed a paw in the center of Catriona's face.

Perfect.

"Is that ye?" asked Broch.

"*No.* It's the dog."

"You're awake?"

She rolled her eyes. "No. I'm talking in my sleep."

You're not the only one who can be sarcastic, you plaid-wearing pain in the—

Broch rolled to his side, and she turned her head to face

him. She could see the moon reflected in his eyes, its light shadowing the curve of his cheekbone. The corner of his mouth twitched into a smile, and the shadows spilled into the dimple created there.

He still smelled like soap.

He must have lathered up and then sat there for hours.

"*What*?" she asked, unnerved by his gaze.

"I think I'd lik' tae kiss ye noo."

She lifted to her elbow. "What?"

"I'd lik' tae put mah lips on yers. Mibbe smoosh them aroond a bit."

She narrowed her eyes.

"I thought I was too *plain*."

"Whit?"

"Back at the apartment. You said I was *plain*."

He laughed. "Och. Na. Ah said that tae bother ye. And—"

"And what?"

"And, my Mother Rose told me if I wanted a lassie, the best way tae dae it was to pretend ah *dinnae* want her."

"She told you to play hard to get?"

"Aye."

"Smart lady."

"Aye."

She frowned. "So that's how you get all the girls?"

He licked his lips and placed his fingertips on her hand.

"Na. I never wanted tae try it before noo."

His sincerity caught her off-guard. It was probably another well-practiced line, but...

Why does he have to be so adorable?

She slid her hand out from under his and placed her fingers on top. "And now you want to *kiss* me."

"Aye."

"Because you asked."

"Aye."

"And you think I'll say yes because I want to kiss you, too."

He shrugged. "I dinnae ken why you'd say *yes* if ye didn't."

Fair point.

She chewed her lip.

"Okay."

He reached out and brushed her cheek with his thumb and then paused. "*Okay* means aye, aye?"

She nodded. "Aye."

He dropped his hand to her waist. Closing her eyes, she felt the heat of his lips brush by her own, and a shiver of expectation ran through her body.

No kiss came.

Grazing her skin, his lips moved across her cheek to her neck. He paused there, his breath warm against her skin.

Mouth moving toward her ear, she heard him whisper.

"I told ye, ye wanted to kiss me."

She gasped.

He rolled back laughing, body quaking with mirth.

Rage and embarrassment devoured the titillation her body had roiled with a moment before.

"You son of a—"

Before she could finish the sentence, he rose to his side again. His lips pressed hard against hers, and he kissed her, her lips, her cheek, her neck. His arms encircled her and pressed her body tighter to his.

She forgot to breathe and gasped to recover as his lips moved beneath her ear.

A tiny voice in her head urged her to pay him back, to tell him she didn't want his attentions, to roll away laughing at him—

She stomped that tiny voice to death until all she could hear was the sound of their breathing.

She threw back her head to allow him easier access to her throat.

He dragged his tongue from the V-notch of her throat to her jaw with the fervor of a starving vampire.

She could feel the want in him—a man possessed. Was it such a stretch that he might be a demon when he'd already traveled through time?

At that moment, she found it hard to care.

His lips traced her jaw until their mouths found each other again, and her hands reached down to cup his backside, demanding his hips move closer to hers. She felt his excitement and his hands moved to cradle her breast. His thumb brushed across her nipple, and she heard a moan. It took a moment for her to realize it was her own.

It's been so long.

He knelt and fumbled with his jeans as she ached with the need for him to master the art of unbuttoning modern apparel.

That's when the poodle on her side of the kilt stretched her leg with a jerk, passed through Catriona's legs, and donkey-kicked Broch in the crotch.

"*Oof!*"

He curled, hands dropping to his crotch.

She realized what had happened and slapped her hand across her mouth.

His eyes widened, lips puckering into an 'O' of pain as he flopped sideways, cupping himself, eyes squinted tight.

"Oh no," she said, knowing the statement was more for her frustrations but hoping he'd take it as sympathy. "That looked like it hurt."

He opened one eye. "Ye hae na idea."

Broch rose to his hands and knees, glaring at the dog, who had already gone back to sleep.

"Where did Lulu git these creatures? Did she agree tae watch the devil's own, in exchange fae some gift?"

Catriona giggled. "That would explain a lot."

"What are ye laughing aboot? It isnae funny."

She tried to force down the corners of her mouth but seeing an embarrassed grin creep across his face, she abandoned the effort and burst into laughter.

Sitting up, she put her hand on his long fingers, which splayed against the tartan as they supported his weight.

"Are you all right?" she asked.

He nodded and held her gaze. "I'm braw."

"I'll assume that means *good*." As she leaned forward to kiss him, she saw his attention shift toward the ridge of the hollow.

Only then did she realize the sun had begun to rise. A subtle glow filled the sky.

"What do you see?"

He kissed her on the tip of her nose and rolled back to sit on his heels.

"Ah think ah hae an idea."

She grimaced. "About us?"

"Na, aboot how tae git tae the house."

She nodded.

"I was afraid of that."

CHAPTER TWENTY-SEVEN

Broch stood and strode a few feet into the forest, adjusting his jeans as he walked. The poodles sat up to watch him with some interest. He studied the ground as he moved as if he were following tracks.

"There are marks here," he said, pointing beside a stump.

Catriona followed. As she arrived beside him, she saw the stump holding his attention did appear suspicious. Leaves seemed glued to the side of it. Scrape marks marred the dirt beside it. Rapping her knuckles on the wood, it returned with a hollow thud.

She gasped. "It isn't *real*."

Broch squatted and fingered what looked like moss on the side of the tree. "Tis on the wrong side. Should be tae the north." He motioned behind him, "Ah've seen signs of wheel-tracks all along, but it looks as though they end here."

He jerked the stump toward the scrape marks, and it slid easily on rails, revealing a hole and a metal ladder leading into the depths. Peering inside, Catriona saw lights.

"There are working lights in the tunnel. I bet it leads to Thorn's house. He must use it to move drugs from the airport without being seen."

Brock smiled. "Then we've found our way intae his castle."

Catriona wasn't as sure all their problems had been solved. "Don't you think the tunnel will be guarded?"

"Only when Thorn is home, and ye said he shouldnae be home yet."

"True. But the house lights were on last night."

"Still are. Could be they always are," he said, standing and peering across the valley as the sun began to rise. She, too, saw Thorn's lights still burned.

One of the dogs bumped up against her in a quest to sniff the tunnel.

Catriona sighed.

"What are we going to do with you two?" she asked them.

Broch tapped a mud stain on top of one dog's head. "At least ah can tell them apart noo. Muddy and Nae Sae Muddy."

Broch stepped onto the ladder and shimmied down. Catriona ran back to where they'd attempted to sleep, balled up the kilt, stuffed it in her bag, and returned. A moment later, Broch called up.

"It looks clear the length as far as ah kin see."

She dropped the luggage down the hole, and he caught it. A moment later, he climbed back up and grabbed one of the confused dogs to transport it into the tunnel. He returned to grab the next, and Catriona followed them down.

At the bottom of the ladder, she saw the tunnel following the curve toward the house. There were tracks on the ground and a string of bulbs lighting the way every fifteen feet or so.

"Ye stay back and let me forge ahead," said Broch.

No sooner did he finish his sentence than both dogs tore down the tunnel after each other, weaving back and forth like ghosts in the dim light.

Catriona put her hands on her hips. "Looks like you were out-voted."

They walked with the dogs in the lead. The poodles started a game—falling back to check on them and then racing forward again until they reached the end of the tunnel. A minecart sat at the bottom of another metal-runged ladder.

"This must lead to the house," whispered Catriona.

Broch nodded. "Aye. Makes sense."

He climbed to the top and placed his ear against a wooden

portal there. After listening for a minute, he pushed open the door, peeked around, and then crawled topside with little delay.

Catriona crouched with a dog under each arm, her stomach in knots.

Broch's face appeared at the top of the ladder.

"Empty," he reported. "Come up and hae a keek."

Catriona considered the dogs, who stood staring up the ladder, tongues lolling.

"What about the dogs?"

"Leave them there. Hard tae hide paw prints all o'er the floors."

She patted the dogs on their heads. "Sorry, kids. You wait here where it's safe."

She climbed the ladder and joined him in what appeared to be an unfinished basement. The floor was dirt, but for a cement platform where an ancient washer and dryer sat, caked with soap. By the light of a small window, she saw a chair in the corner. Behind it, four shackles hung from the walls.

For Sean?

"That can't be good," she said, motioning to the chains. "On the upside, if they're for Sean, it means Thorn planned to bring him back alive."

Grim-faced, Broch wandered over to study a brown stain on the cement wall.

"Ah dinnae think Sean will be the first," he said.

Catriona spotted a small bucket sitting on a rusted metal shelf and used the laundry sink to fill it before scurrying it down to the dogs. The poodles, exhausted from their adventure, had already curled up for a nap, but they stood to drink.

"Good kids," said Catriona, patting them.

She returned to the basement. From there, she and Broch took the stairs to the door leading into the home. Catriona noticed Broch's boots sitting on the top stair.

"Tak' aff yer shoes," he directed.

She complied, and they slipped into the main house.

Thorn's oversized cabin was large but unadorned with any homey touches. The living room held little more than a television and large L-shaped sofa, patches of it worn away to expose the foam cushions within. Beer cans littered the tabletops. The three bedrooms had two or three single beds apiece, but for one with a king. Plates piled high in the sink.

"Looks like they left in a hurry. I felt cleaner in the forest." Catriona's nose wrinkled at the sight of the filth. "We need to set up an ambush."

Broch pulled at his stubbled chin. "Aye. Tis whit ah'm thinking."

Catriona and Broch moved through the house, searching closets and cabinets for weapons. Catriona found an untouched family-sized bag of candy bars in the kitchen and took it. From the refrigerator, she stole a half-eaten leftover cheesesteak for the poodles and a block of remarkably fresh-looking cheese.

Broch cocked an eyebrow at her as she carted her spoils to the middle of the living room.

"Hae ye been to market?" he asked.

She tore open the plastic bag and thrust a candy bar at him. "We need to *eat*. Here, stuff this in your mouth."

He inspected the wrapper, peeled it away, and took a dainty bite. His eyes lit.

"That's *magic*," he said, taking another, much larger chomp.

"I thought you'd like it."

Catriona returned to searching for weapons. Closing the closet door on their last hope, she leaned against the wall.

"How can there be no guns in a drug dealer's den? You'd think this place would have them piled to the rafters."

Broch grunted his agreement through the wad of chocolate and peanuts in his mouth.

Catriona peeled a candy bar of her own. "I knew I should have brought my gun. I didn't think I could get it on the flight, but in hindsight, why would I think it would be a problem on *Lulu's* lawless plane?"

The sound of engines roaring outside kept her from lamenting their situation for long.

She gathered up the things she'd stolen from the kitchen,

and the two of them flanked the front window, backs to the wall. Peering through the yellowed curtains, Catriona saw three ATVs roll to a stop, feet from the front door. One had an open bed in the back, and from her angle, she saw a man lying on his side inside it.

"They have Sean," she whispered.

Broch had his eye to the window as well, and he nodded.

"We cannae make our stand here noo," he whispered back to her. "There are tae many of them."

She agreed. They were unarmed, and in addition to Thorn and the two men she recognized from California, another had joined the group.

Broch motioned toward the door leading to the basement. "We need tae go back to the tunnel, *noo*."

Catriona knew he was right, but it was hard to leave with Sean right outside, so clearly in distress.

"What about Sean?" she asked.

"Na time." He grabbed her wrist and tugged her toward the hall.

"But they could kill him before—"

"If they haven't yet, they willnae noo."

Again, she knew the Highlander was correct. There would be little sense in dragging Sean across the country just to kill him the moment they arrived at their lair.

Catriona and Broch grabbed their shoes and scurried back to the basement. They slipped into the tunnel just as boots echoed on the floor above.

The poodles greeted them with excited spins and leaps. Catriona petted them to keep them calm while Broch worked the trapdoor shut behind them.

With the door sealed, Broch slid down the ladder.

"We can't call the police," said Catriona, running through their options in her head. "It would turn into a standoff and probably end with Sean dead."

Broch nodded. "Agreed. And they're probably being bribed, as well."

She nodded. Thorn operated in plain view of the locals,

which didn't bode well for their chances of finding an honest local police force.

Even a man from the seventeen hundreds knew that.

It seemed, in many ways, things hadn't changed much from Kilty's time to hers.

"We could go back to town. Get armed?"

Broch tilted his head from side to side. "Ah dinnae. It's still two against five. Ah'm nae sure we want a gunfight."

"But we'd have the element of surprise."

"They'd hae numbers, guns, and a *prisoner*."

Catriona groaned. Everything came back to Sean. At any point, all Thorn had to do was shoot him—or *threaten* to shoot him—and the war would be lost.

They had some time, but they needed to devise a plan.

"What does Thorn have planned for Sean?" she wondered aloud. "Why drag him across the country?"

Broch slid to a squat, his back against the wall. His eyes were locked on Catriona, but she could tell his thoughts had wandered far away.

"They'll keep him," he said.

"Hm?"

His gaze shifted to the trapdoor. "The hoose wasn't large, and there are four of them. They willnae give Sean a bed with a comfortable set of irons in the basement."

Her eyes widened. "Of *course*. They'll lock him in those chains, right above our heads." She frowned. "They might have a guard on him..."

Broch shook his head. "Na reason tae keep an old man guarded."

"Probably not. All we have to do is wait and then sneak up and get him."

"Aye. Where force won't work, guile might. We'll pull him intae the tunnel and be gone by the time they ken."

Broch stood, pointing up the ladder. "Ah'm aff tae keep mah ear on the door. If they open it tae find me there, don't wait. Ye run down the tunnel like a rabbit."

She shook her head. "I can't make any promises. We'll see."

He scowled and poked his index finger in her face. "Ye better listen tae me, lassie. I willnae hae yer blood on mah hands."

She scoffed. "I'm the one who brought you here. I'm the one who'll have blood on her hands."

She eased his finger away with her own and leaned her face toward his. "Keep the heid, Kilty."

He chuckled and tapped her nose with his finger. "Keep the heid."

He grabbed the ladder rung with one hand and shook a fist playfully at her with the other.

"You're aff tae be a burr beneath mah saddle. Ah can *tell*."

CHAPTER TWENTY-EIGHT

Sean did his best to walk under his own power as Thorn's goon led him from the bed of the all-terrain vehicle to the house. His legs felt like noodles. *Achy* noodles. Folding a sixty-something-year-old body into the trunk of a car for two days could do that.

They'd arrived at a large cabin in the woods. Sean noted with dismay there'd be no running to the neighbors for help. Nothing but trees stretched in every direction.

Inside the house, his escort shoved him toward a sofa, and he fell into it, shoulder first. His hands were still tied behind his back. He righted himself and pushed a fingernail into the tip of each of his fingers in turn, both happy and surprised to discover he could still feel them.

Having deposited Sean, the man beelined for the kitchen. The staccato sound of slamming kitchen cabinets filled the air.

"There's no food," said someone.

"Where are my candy bars?" said another voice.

The drive had wreaked havoc on Thorn's aging frame and he limped through the front door on unsteady feet. He stretched his back, using his cane for balance. His crooked features seemed even more offset, the skin beneath his left eye sagging.

"Go get food," he barked.

"What?" asked the man with the lump on his forehead as he appeared behind Thorn. Sean had heard someone call him Knotty.

"*Food*. Go get some," repeated Thorn.

Knotty scowled. "Me?"

"All of you."

"We shouldn't leave you here alone—"

Thorn twisted to face him.

"You think I can't handle myself alone with a tied-up old man?"

"No. I mean, yeah, you can, I just—"

"I need some time alone with him. *Go get some food.* All of ye."

Knotty ran a hand over his head. "Right. Sure, Thorn. We'll get some food. But I'm leaving Clint outside here, just in case."

Thorn sighed. "Fine."

The others filed outside, and Sean heard the ATVs roar to life. The sound of the engines grew fainter until he and Thorn remained, staring at each other in silence.

Sean adjusted to a more seated position. With a grunt, Thorn hobbled to a faux leather recliner and lowered his bulky frame into it. He slid a handgun from his waistband and set it on the torn arm of the chair.

His gaze settled on Sean, and he cleared his throat.

"Take me to the future," he said.

Sean's brow knit. "What?"

"Take me to the future. They don't have what I need here."

"What is it you need?"

"A cure."

"For what? Cancer?"

Thorn guffawed. "I *wish*."

Sean watched with fascination as the big man thrust two stubby fingers into his mouth and moved them around as if he was searching for the last olive in a jar.

He heard a *pop!* and the entire left side of Thorn's face collapsed.

Gagging, Thorn jerked a white object from his mouth, spit dripping from it to his lap. Sean noted the row of teeth along its edge.

His whole jaw?

"That's quite a trick," said Sean.

"It's how I get all the ladies," croaked Thorn, the words almost impossible to recognize, tumbling past the loose flesh of Thorn's face.

Thorn slipped the prosthetic back into place, wincing with pain. Restored, he took a moment to find his composure and continued.

"The same thing that took my jaw took my leg, my arm, and half my face. I could pop out this eye and play marbles with it."

Sean frowned. "Please don't."

"My whole body is Swiss cheese." Thorn pulled down his shirt, and Sean saw his chest was riddled with stained bandages. "This thing would have killed a lesser man. But it made me stronger. Gave me the strength I needed to do the things I've done. To build my empire here."

Sean nodded. "I don't know what any of that has to do with me."

"In the last few years, it's become less about dealin' with the pain and more about stayin' alive. No doctor has ever seen anything like it, and I've been to them all. I can live without a leg or an arm, but it's my insides now—it's like somethin's eatin' me. A little more disappears every day, and whatever the monster is, it's getting *hungrier*. Feeding faster. There's no rot. No infection. They can't stop it because *there ain't nothin' there*."

Thorn leaned forward before continuing. "But you knew that, didn't you, Ryft? You know I don't have any ordinary disease. I could tell the first time you laid eyes on me, you weren't surprised to see me this way."

Sean looked out the front window, wondering how long it would take the others to get food. Them being gone might be his best chance of escaping.

"There's no hope for you in the future, Thorn. Quite the opposite," he said.

Thorn slammed his fist against his thigh, and Sean heard the hollow sound of a leg *not* made of flesh. "The future'll have a cure. Take me far enough forward, and *someone* will have found a cure."

Sean shook his head. "There's no cure."

"There *is*. There *must* be."

"There's not. The problem is simple." Sean returned his attention to Thorn, whose chin glistened with drool. "You're not supposed to be here."

"No *shit*." Thorn barked a mirthless laugh. "I didn't ask to come here. This was your doin'."

"It was an accident."

Thorn leaned back and took several long, deep breaths, composing himself before he continued.

"Don't get me wrong, Sean. I'd be dead already if I were back home. That I'm here is the only thing that saved me." He touched his jaw with the tips of his fingers. "They don't have 3D printers for making jawbones in seventeen twenty-one. They don't have mechanical legs and synthetic skin in the ancient Highlands."

Sean sighed. "No. But seventeen twenty-one had something this time doesn't have."

"What's that?"

"*You*. And it wants to keep you."

Thorn waved his hand like he was swatting a fly. "What does that mean? You're talkin' gibberish."

"It means you're not fit to travel through time. Your body wants to go back where it belongs. And it is one atom at a time."

Thorn's lips parted, and he stared at Sean for several beats as if he were processing this new information.

"I think I know what you're sayin'," he began, waggling a finger in Sean's direction. "I've always felt a—*a pull*. You're sayin' it's *time*? Trying to pull me back where I belong?"

Sean nodded. "I'm surprised you've lasted this long."

"But what about you? You look fit."

"I was made to travel this way."

"Made?" Thorn scowled. "What are ye? Some kind of alien?"

Sean chuckled. "I don't think so."

Thorn rocked forward to get up. He made it as far as the edge of the seat and then paused to thrust an index finger in

Sean's direction.

"You brought me here to kill me. You knew you couldn't beat me in a fair fight."

Sean shook his head. "I told you, it was an accident. I didn't *choose* to bring you. You pushed a sword through my lung. When I'm near death, the jump heals me. Somehow we were too entangled: you traveled forward with me."

Thorn hung his head, panting, his breath ragged. As the rise and fall of his chest steadied, he looked back up at Sean.

"Then take me *back*."

"What?"

"Take me back where I belong so that I can be reunited with the rest of my body."

Sean sighed. "That's not how it works. Even if I could take you back—and I can't—it wouldn't make you whole. You'd be as you are now and with nothing but eighteenth-century medicine to ease your pain. I wouldn't wish that on, well, *you*."

Thorn's face grew red with anger. "Then, the *future*, as I said. They'll know what to do."

"I'm telling you, there's no cure for being out of time."

Thorn roared, spittle flying.

"How do you know?"

Sean hung his head. "I know."

Thorn wiped his mouth on the back of his hand. "I should kill you now. Get up."

Sean stood.

Thorn used his cane to stand and retrieved his handgun to point at Sean.

"Walk. To that door on the right."

"Thorn. Listen to me. There's no reason—"

"Go!" Thorn poked him with the gun, the veins in his forehead threatening to burst.

Sean walked to the door.

"Open it."

"I can't. My hands are tied."

"I've spent decades with half my body missing. Figure it out."

Sean turned his back to the door and twisted the knob with his tied hands. Righting himself, he pushed the door open the rest of the way with his foot. Stairs led downward.

"Go," said Thorn, waggling the gun toward the basement.

Sean followed the stairs into a dirt-floored basement. A single chair sat in the corner, iron chains hanging from the wall behind it.

"Sit."

Sean walked to the chair and sat. "Killing me isn't going to change anything."

Thorn stood six feet away, the gun in his hand shaking as if the exertion of walking down the stairs had exhausted his reserves.

"Will it change anything when I call your son?" he asked.

Sean fought the urge to react. "I don't know what you're talking about."

"How stupid do you think I am? That boy is the spitting image of ye. And since he appeared in a kilt, I'm thinking he's a time traveler, too? Am I right? I wonder what poor bastard he brought with him to this cursed time."

Sean remained silent.

"Want to deny he's yours? What if I told you I have the girl's phone number? Is she your daughter? She comes from the past as well?" Thorn scowled. "I think not. But she's precious enough to you, of that I'm sure."

Sean looked away. "Stop wasting my time. You're boring me with all your *poor me* whining—"

"I'm not *whining*." Thorn coughed, struggling to keep his gun raised. Sean suspected he'd lost lung tissue. Could be time pulling him back, could be the cigarettes he'd smelled from the trunk. Thorn was dying either way. It didn't matter how, except it wasn't happening fast enough for him.

This is my chance.

Sean lowered his head and charged the man. Thorn cracked him in the skull with his weapon before he could reach him. Unable to deflect the blow or keep his balance with his hands bound behind him, Sean collapsed to the floor.

Thorn kept the gun pointed at him as he wrestled his coughing fit under control.

"Get back in the chair," he croaked.

Sean rose and sat.

Thorn continued, his voice hoarse.

"As I was sayin', I'm gonna call your boy and your girl and tell them where they can find you. When they get here—when your son is tied up beside you, and your girl is upstairs with my boys—*then* we'll see if you can think of a way to help me."

Sean felt a surge of rage rush through him.

"I told you, there's nothing I can do. *Nothing.*"

Thorn took a wobbly step forward, his sweat dripping down his cheeks.

"Can you even imagine the *pain?*" he asked. "Imagine your nerves, disappearing, *exposed*, each played like the devil's own fiddle? I'm going to make sure those kids of yours feel every *bit* of the pain I've endured. You have no idea what I've done to survive."

Impassioned, Thorn raised his hand to the sky.

Sean's rage hit a crescendo. He leaped from his chair, this time staying low, and speared his foe in the stomach with his head.

The gun went off.

Sean felt pain radiating through his chest.

He stumbled back and fell into the chair.

CHAPTER TWENTY-NINE

The man in the dark hood spurred his horse and galloped back toward Mother Margaret's house.

Brochan stood, transfixed by the sight of the man rising and falling on his steed, up and down, like the beating of a black heart.

Keep the heid.

He heard Mother Margaret's voice so clearly that he turned to see if she'd walked out of the house.

Of course, she hadn't. Her hands had been cold as ice.

Keep the heid.

He spun, plucked his sword from the belly of the dead man, and held it high.

The hooded man reached across his body and pulled his sword, much larger than Brochan's.

He was nearly upon him.

Keep the heid.

Heart beating twice as fast as the horse's hooves, Broch bent his knees and lowered his sword as if submitting to his fate.

The hooded man was twenty feet away from him.

Ten.

He could see the steam and snot sputtering from the horse's nostrils.

Five.

Keep the heid.

He sprung.

Thrusting with all his might, Broch leaped upward, his sword leading the attack.

The man caught the blade as if it were nothing more than a flower stem.

Broch felt his whole body jerk upward, his face meeting the side of the man's sword with such force he thought his skull would pop open like an oyster shell.

He felt the blade split the flesh from above to below his eye socket, and, flung by the bulk of the horse, Broch flew through the air. He landed on his back. The breath in his lungs expelled with one great rush.

Brock sat up, gasping for air, blood streaming down his face.

The man pulled up his horse and slid off. He bolted toward Brochan as if he had only moments to kill the boy, sword held high above his head.

The man's glove had been torn away when he grabbed Brochan's sword. The flesh on his hand hung, exposed, and ragged.

There was no blood.

Brochan saw a flash of metal in the sunlight as if the bones in the man's hand were carved from silver.

A metal man?

Before he could make sense of what he saw, there was a burst of light. Brochan turned his head, shielding the eye not already blinded by blood. He felt weightless. It reminded him of a time he'd been thrown by his pony, flying through the air, the unnatural and exhilarating feel of moving *upward*.

Somewhere, the metal man released an anguished scream, but it sounded very far away.

"Wake up!"

Brochan opened his eyes to find Catriona tapping his skull with her foot. A dog lay in his lap, the poodle's body rising and falling as she slept.

He remembered Catriona had offered to listen for signs of

Sean, to give him a chance to rest. It wasn't easy hanging from the ladder, ear pressed to a trapdoor, and he'd agreed to take a quick break. Now, she hung from one of the rungs, kicking him in the head with the toe of her boot.

"Ah fell asleep?"

"Shhh. Don't worry about that. I think they took Sean to the basement. I hear voices."

Broch stood, sliding the poodle from his body. "Move. Let me up."

"Wait. I'm *listening*," she hissed.

"Let me up. If something happens, ah'm strong enough tae open the door and get up there."

She glared down at him, her eyes aflame with determination, before finally relenting.

"Fine. Be *quiet*. I think they're right above our heads."

He stepped back to let her drop to the floor and then scurried up the rungs. He was almost to the top when the sudden sound of a gunshot nearly made him fall.

The dogs yipped.

Catriona gasped and then squatted to pull the dogs to her, trying to settle them.

Broch locked eyes with her.

"*Run*," he said before slamming the trapdoor with his palm.

A second blast exploded.

Broch slipped back down a rung as a bullet struck the open door above his head.

"*Broch!*" called Catriona from below him.

Broch once again hauled himself upward and popped his head from the hole like a gopher. He caught a glimpse of Thorn, sitting on the ground, gun in hand.

Sean was there. He sat at an odd angle, his back against the chair they'd seen earlier. Even in the dim light, Broch could see blood staining his shirt.

Thorn swiveled his gun to point it at Sean.

"Hold it there, or I'll kill him," he said.

Broch shook his head.

"*Na.*"

He leaped from his spot on the ladder and into the basement. Thorn fired at him as he dodged, missing.

Lucky.

Broch shifted direction and charged.

Before Thorn could fire a second time, he tackled the man, forcing his aim away from Sean's still body. Another shot rang out. A bullet struck the ceiling. Broch knocked away the gun, and it skittered across the dirt toward the stairs.

Straddling Thorn, Broch swung. The big man's cheekbone collapsed beneath the force of his blow as if his face was made of paper.

Reaching up, Thorn grasped Broch's shirt, his eyes wide with what looked like both fury and fear. His jaw worked in its ragged path, but Broch heard nothing but a wet, gurgling breath.

Another gun blast exploded in the shallow basement.

Broch covered his head.

Feeling nothing strike him, he peered from beneath his arm to find Catriona at the bottom of the stairs, Thorn's gun in her hand. Her attention was locked somewhere above him, and he looked up the stairs leading into the house.

A second handgun tumbled down the steps and dropped to the dirt beside him.

A man's body collapsed at the top of the steps.

Broch turned to Catriona, and a voice said the thing he'd been thinking.

"Good shot."

It was Sean's voice. His old man's eyes were open. Turning his attention from Catriona to Broch, he spoke in a slow staccato.

"There are more. They'll be back. We need to go."

"Is he dead?" asked Catriona, motioning to Thorn, as she checked the pulse of the fallen henchman.

Broch picked up the soldier's gun and used it to poke at Thorn. The big man didn't move, nor did he appear to be breathing. His face had collapsed into itself.

Sean struggled to sit up, and Broch jumped to his feet to

assist. He tried to remove the ties on Sean's wrists but found the material unusually strong.

"Check his pockets," said Sean, nodding toward Thorn.

Broch did so and retrieved an item. He showed it to Sean, hoping it was something useful.

"It's a pocket knife. It opens," said Catriona. She plucked the object from his hands. Opening it, she cut the bands on Sean's wrists and threw her arms around her adopted father.

Broch watched the old man wince.

"I thought I'd never see you again," she said.

Sean offered a lopsided smile. "You know you can't get rid of me."

Broch kept an eye on Thorn as he helped Sean to his feet.

"What about him?"

Rubbing his arms, Sean looked down on his old foe. Thorn's body had gone slack, his eyes glazed.

"He's dead, lad. Leave him. He drowned in his own face."

Catriona winced. *"What?"*

Broch noticed blood soaking Sean's shirt. He reached out and stuck his finger through a hole in the fabric there.

"Yer shot?"

Sean glanced down. "Not mortally."

"Are ye sure?"

Sean chuckled.

"If I were dying, we wouldn't be having this conversation."

CHAPTER THIRTY

Broch, Catriona, and Sean escaped back down the tunnel. When they arrived back at the airport, Sean insisted they contact the authorities.

Catriona didn't love the idea. She suggested they head home and pretend they'd never been there, but Sean insisted on doing everything *right.*

So infuriating.

Luckily, if the local police force was corrupt, their loyalties to Thorn had died with him. Unfortunately, they *did* insist Catriona, Broch, and Sean stay in nearby Knoxville while they sorted the mess at Thorn's hideaway.

With Sean's blessing, Catriona told the police Thorn had kidnapped Sean in an attempt to muscle his way into the Hollywood drug scene. They had time traveling the tunnel to concoct the story.

Since Thorn was the best-known drug dealer in the county, no one doubted the story. The ligature marks on Sean's wrists and ankles, as well as the bloodstains on his chest, went far toward convincing them the kidnapping story was true.

Which it was. More or less.

The EMTs tended to the wound in Sean's chest—high and far enough to the left to avoid major damage—and took him to the hospital in the back of an ambulance, much to Sean's chagrin.

Catriona and Broch left with the police, squeezing into the back seat of a cruiser with the poodles. As they tumbled out of the car at the station, a man in a black suit walked up and thrust out a hand.

"I'll take the dogs," he said.

Catriona looked down at the leashes in her hand and then back at the man.

"Who are you?"

He sniffed. "Miss Lulu sent me."

Catriona handed over the leashes. The man walked off, dogs prancing on either side of him.

Catriona side-eyed Broch.

"Why are we about to spend the next three hours in a police station, and the dogs are off in a private car to have baths and dinner?"

Broch shrugged. "They're very fancy dogs."

Catriona dug out her phone and called Lulu to tell her what a disaster the actresses' poor planning had nearly been for the dogs.

The star offered little more than a grunting noise, which *could* have been mistaken for an apology.

Catriona took what she could get.

They tromped into the station for their obligatory questioning.

Catriona hoped they planned to question them *together*. They were already walking a tightrope—the last thing she needed was Broch acting as if he'd just stepped off the set of *Outlander*. They'd arrest them on principal.

As they rounded a corner toward the interrogation rooms, the officer in the lead guided Broch to the left. Another took her to the right.

She swore under her breath.

Then she sat.

For *hours*.

She answered questions as truthfully as possible—based around the agreed story of Thorn's Hollywood drug-trade takeover attempt—hoping Broch did the same.

By the time she was done, she could barely keep her eyes open. Her body felt coated in a sheet of grime. Her muscles ached. She knew she looked as if she'd been tossed to the curb after a three a.m. bar closing.

When she finally stepped into the hall, she heard laughter. Squinting beneath the fluorescent lights, she spotted two officers walking toward her, laughing as if they'd been in that same bar, having the time of their lives.

One turned down the hall, revealing a third man behind them.

Kilty.

The remaining officer clapped Broch on the back before heading down the hall with his friend.

"I'll see you, Broch."

The man could barely contain his amusement.

Broch saw her and grinned.

"Hey, there ye are," he said, looking fresh as a daisy.

She scowled.

Charming bastard.

CHAPTER THIRTY-ONE

Following the interviews, the police drove Broch and Catriona out of Campbell County and dropped them off at a Knoxville hotel to keep them far from retaliation by Thorn's gang. They promised to protect them until they were on a plane headed for California.

After over twenty-four hours—on a plane, sleeping in the woods, running through a tunnel, and rotting in a police station—all Catriona wanted was a hot shower and a long night's sleep.

Her brain swirled with images from the day before. It didn't help Broch couldn't stop asking questions about the police, television, hospitals—everything he spotted that didn't exist in the eighteenth century. He was especially fascinated by the police sirens and red and blue flashing lights—which the officers, of course, let him play with on the drive to the hotel.

They didn't think twice about Broch's naiveté—apparently, they assumed *everyone* from Scotland lived in what amounted to the eighteenth century.

By the time they reached the hotel, she'd forbidden the Highlander to ask any more questions.

"Same room?" asked the desk clerk, checking them in.

Unsure she had a choice, she glanced at the officer by her side.

He shrugged.

"It'll make it easier for us to protect you," he said, then he looked past her and winked at Broch.

She saw it.

Catriona turned to a grinning Broch, who quickly sobered and stared up at the television hanging from the wall in the lobby as if he'd never seen one before.

She scowled.

Uh-huh.

She didn't have the energy to fight and didn't see the point of separate rooms. They were *adults*, after all.

Broch's chin dropped in awe as a cartoon played on the screen.

Well, *she* was an adult.

"Could we do two queens?" she asked.

The woman behind the counter nodded and typed away on her keyboard.

Catriona retrieved the key cards and headed for their room, grabbing Broch's arm as she passed him.

The officer followed them into the elevator.

"So the queen slept here?" asked Broch as they rode the elevator to the seventeenth floor.

She squinted at him. "What?"

"The lassie said we hae *the queen's bed.*"

The officer snorted a laugh.

Catriona sighed. "Queen is a *size* of bed. Beds can be twin, full, queen, or king-size."

"But—"

She shook a scolding finger at him.

"No more questions. Remember?"

"Aye. Sorry." He put his hand over his mouth to show his restraint.

The officer chuckled again.

Catriona tilted her head back and closed her eyes.

I am going to fall asleep on my feet.

"Hm," grunted Broch as the elevator doors opened. "How did we get from where we were to—"

Catriona paused to put her finger over his lips.

He scowled.

The three of them walked into the hallway to search for the room. Broch grunted and then grunted again until she could take it no more. She whirled to face him.

"*What*? Why do you keep making that noise?"

He waved her away. "Och, 'tis nothing."

"Then *stop*."

"Aye."

She located the door and slid the card through the reader. The lights flashed red, and Broch grunted again.

She rested her forehead on the door. Summoning strength, she ran the key card again.

The lights flashed green.

There is a God.

She pushed inside. Broch high-fived the officer, and then they left him in the hall.

Catriona closed the door.

Broch grunted.

She whirled.

"What? *Just say it.*"

He opened his expression, looking as innocent as a child.

"Whit?"

"What do you want to know?"

"Och, it's just—ah was thinking—shouldn't it be *prince or princess* bed, queen, and king? Whatfur *twin*?"

She squinted. "What?"

"The *beds*." He pulled at his chin. "Or, dae yer king and queen hae twins?"

Catriona dropped her head into her hand.

I should have gotten two rooms.

She turned to him. "You're wondering about the name of the bed sizes?"

"Aye."

She took a deep breath. "Twin beds come in pairs; that's why they're called *twin*. None of it has anything to do with actual kings and queens, and we don't have either, anyway. We have *presidents*."

"Presidents," he echoed.

She nodded. "Presidents. Okay?"

Setting down the bag of necessities she'd bought at the hotel store, she opened the shades and took a moment to study the minibar offerings.

By the time she straightened, Broch had disappeared.

"Where did you—"

"They should probably call them *president* beds then, don't you think?"

It sounded as if Broch's voice rang from an echo chamber. She heard the sound of running water and realized he was already in the shower.

"Who said you get a shower first?" she shouted at the partially closed bathroom door.

"Hey, howfur did ye open the door with that little white rectangle?" he called back.

Catriona released a frustrated scream and peeled back the top cover of one of the beds. She flopped down on it, plotting her revenge.

Catriona smiled. She felt warm and cozy. Something smelled *amazing*, like lemon and basil. Her fingers touched something soft and fuzzy wrapped around her waist.

She opened her eyes.

The morning sun shone through the drapes. Looking down, she realized the furry wrap around her waist was Broch's arm, and his hand cupped her breast.

For the love of...

She heard his steady breathing and felt it ruffling her hair.

I'm the little spoon.

He was tucked under the covers, but she'd fallen asleep on top. She pulled away from him and tumbled out of bed. Broch's eyes popped open, and he lifted his fist, ready to repel attackers.

His eyes focused on her, and he grinned.

"Good morning, lassie."

"Why the hell are you in my bed?"

"Hm?"

She motioned to the other queen. "We have two beds for a *reason*."

He shrugged. "Ah found ye asleep on top of the covers. Ah was keeping ye warm. The poodles weren't here ta dae it."

She sighed. Hard logic with which to argue.

She realized she still felt *gross*. She'd fallen asleep before getting a shower. The air had smelled sweet when she was covered in *Broch*. Now, away from his soap overdose, she smelled only herself, and it wasn't good.

She rubbed her eyes. "I can't believe I fell asleep. What time is it?" She looked at the clock and saw it was seven-thirty. "We have to find Sean."

"Aye." He stretched and rolled onto his back beneath the covers.

She noted the pitch of a tent where his crotch area lay and twisted her lips to the right. "You're naked under there, aren't you."

He put his hand over the lump. "Aye. Sorry. That happens in the morn. It tisn't ye."

"Oh, well, *gosh*, thanks."

"I mean ah'm not trying tae bother ye."

She caught another whiff of forest and tunnel.

"I stink," she mumbled.

He nodded. "That's whit ah'm *saying*..."

She jerked the pillow off the other queen bed and threw it at him.

He deflected it, laughing.

Catriona checked her phone to find a message from Sean, letting her know the hospital had kept him overnight. He would be fine, but his vitals struck the doctors as unusual. He tried to convince them he *always* had odd vitals, but they'd kept him to cure his dehydration, anyway.

When she turned to relay the message to Broch, she

realized he was in the shower again.

She gritted her teeth.

I'm going to smell like a Tennessee tunnel for the rest of my life.

Twenty minutes later, Catriona took her turn in the shower, proud of herself for not screaming at Broch for jumping the line, *again*, when he walked out toweled and smelling even fresher.

The water felt like heaven.

Sure, she had to search for soap when she realized Broch had used all the hotel's, but she found the stash he'd brought with him, and things proceeded as planned.

She finished without incident.

Everything was okay.

Today would be a good day.

Today, they'd head back to California, and everything would be back to—

Catriona stepped out of the shower and stopped.

"Broch?"

The Highlander was nowhere to be seen.

She scowled. He was too big to hide.

She stuck her head into the hall. A new officer looked up at her from his folding chair.

"Hey," he said.

"Hey. Did Broch come this way?"

He nodded. "My partner took him to the hospital."

"Your—why did he go without *me*?"

The officer shrugged.

CHAPTER THIRTY-TWO

"There you are," said Sean when Broch found his hospital room and poked his head inside.

He turned to the officer flanking him.

"Could ye wait here?"

The man nodded and took a spot leaning against the wall next to the door.

Broch entered Sean's room. The old man seemed in good spirits, and the color had returned to his cheeks.

Sean scowled.

"Where's Catriona?"

"Ah sneaked oot while she was in the shower."

"Why? What's wrong?"

Brochan grimaced.

"Ah wanted a moment alone with ye."

Sean nodded. "Okay."

Broch took a deep breath, steeling himself to ask the question that had been burning in his mind for almost two days.

"Yer book said ah was yer son."

Sean swallowed. "You are."

"Howfur dae ye ken?"

Sean's expression softened as he placed a hand on his heart. "I can *feel* it. And you're the spitting image of me when I was your age." He hemmed. "Well, maybe not as handsome—"

Broch scoffed. "Ye hasnae seen me with mah hairspray."

Sean laughed as Broch pulled up a chair, turned it around, and sat on it so he could rest his arms on the back.

"Whit happened? How come did ye leave our time?" he asked.

Sean sighed. "Thorn killed your mother, and I thought *you*, as well. There was a war going on between his people and the ones I swore to protect. I knew Thorn would be there. I found him on the field, and I had him dead to rights—and then—"

His gaze drifted.

"Whit?"

"I heard a voice calling my name. I lost my concentration for a split second, and Thorn ran me clean through with his sword."

"And ye dinnae die?"

"No. Time-traveling heals. I traveled to live. I didn't have any reason to stay, anyway."

"And Thorn came with ye?"

Sean nodded. "It was an accident. Though, it couldn't have happened to a nicer fella. The jump killed him. Slowly, but it did."

"That's what happened to his—" Broch swirled his hand over his face.

Sean nodded.

Broch took a moment to digest the information.

"Ye say time traveling heals?"

"Yes. Haven't you heard? *Time heals all wounds.*" Sean laughed. "I hardly ever get to use that joke."

Broch touched his side. "Time dinnae heal *me*."

Sean frowned. "Ah. I've been wanting to talk to you about that. Do you remember how you were injured?"

Broch shook his head.

"What about your eye? That didn't heal the way it should have either."

Broch touched his scar. "That ah mind. A man on a horse. A man in black who killed mah mothers. Ah think ah was a boy. It came to me in a dream."

"Do you remember what he looked like? The man in black?"

"Na. He wore a hood. But his arm—it was made of metal, *inside*."

"Inside?"

"My sword sliced the flesh of his hand, and beneath was metal."

"And this man cut you across your eye?"

"Aye."

"Then what?"

Broch shrugged. "Ah dinnae remember."

Sean looked away, looking pensive.

"Whit is it?" asked Broch.

Sean sighed. "Time travel doesn't heal the wounds Travelers give each other. But—I don't know who of our people would have attacked you. I killed the last of the traitors. And I don't know who this metal man is. We need to find out before he comes after you again or—"

"*There you are*." Catriona walked in, sending the door swinging, her expression wild with what looked like anger, mixed with a healthy helping of frustration.

"Or *whit*?" Broch shook his father's arm, doing his best to block out Catriona's interruption.

The old man's voice dropped low. "—or *her*."

Broch's eyes grew wide. "You mind he'll come fer Catriona?"

"What are you talking about?" asked Catriona.

"Nothing. It's so good to see you," said Sean, holding out his arms for a hug.

Catriona leaned in, glaring at Broch, even as she hugged the old man.

"Why didn't you wait for me?" she growled as she released Sean.

Broch crossed his arms against his chest.

"Och. Ah cannae wait for ye all day, wummin."

Her eyes popped wide. "Are you kidding me? You kept hogging the shower—" She stopped to poke a finger at him. "And you better watch it with that *wummin* stuff. I'm not one of your tavern wenches."

He scowled. "Whit tavern wenches?"

She held up a palm.

"You know what? I'm not doing this. It's going to be a good day if it *kills* me."

She returned her attention to Sean, smiling sweetly.

"So, they said you're doing well, and we can leave. You have a lot of explaining to do, mister."

Sean nodded. "I'm sure."

"Like, do I have to start calling you Ryft, now?"

Sean chuckled. "I renamed myself *Sean* when I arrived because everyone thought I was Irish."

Catriona pressed on. "But where did—"

Sean placed his hand on hers. "Easy. I have plenty of time to answer all your questions."

She pouted. "But all this leads me to one question I need to ask *now*…"

He grimaced. "Fine. *One*."

She looked from Sean to Broch and back again. "Are you both sticking around for a while? Or should I expect to wake up and find you whisked away through time and space?"

Sean smiled. "We'll be around for a bit. You two are getting along?"

Catriona and Broch exchanged a glance.

"Aye," said Broch.

"Sure," said Catriona.

Broch stuck his tongue out at her.

Catriona replied in kind and then looked away, so he wouldn't have the satisfaction of seeing her giggle.

She shook her head. "I can't *believe* I'm stuck with *two* dirty time travelers."

Broch straightened.

"Ah may be many things," he said, frowning. "But ah'm nae *dirty*."

EPILOGUE

New York, NY

Michael sat up in bed, the sheet sliding off his chest to his waist. The name of a city sang in his mind.

Los Angeles.

Anne stirred beside him.

"Why are you up?" she asked, cracking open an eye. "I thought we agreed to try and sleep."

He scowled. "I had a vision."

"A vision?" She rolled over to better see him. "You're a mystic now?"

He scoffed. "By layman's terms, I always have been."

Anne rolled her eyes. "I swear. You're so full of yourself there's two of you." She sighed. "Okay, I'll bite. What's the vision?"

"There's been a disturbance in Los Angeles."

"So what else is new?"

He frowned. "A *time* disturbance."

"What does that mean?"

Michael hemmed, unsure how much he wanted to share. Anne was his best Sentinel, and his love—two things he would *also* never share with her—but she was, and always would be, on a need-to-know basis when it came to Angeli business.

"We've been aware of another group..." he paused and

started again. "There's a species of time traveler—"

Anne's brow knit. "A *species*? Are we talking people or birds?"

He glowered at her. "*People.*"

She closed her eyes. "Okay. Forget I asked. We just finished defeating the greatest threat to the world...blah, blah blah. I'm over intrigue for a while."

"This could be serious, though."

"Uh-huh."

"I'm going to have to send someone."

"Okay."

"My best..."

Anne's eyes opened and her attention snapped to him.

"*No.*"

"I'm afraid I don't have any choice."

She sat up.

"*No.* C'mon, Michael. You're *killing* me. Don't I deserve a little time off?"

"You do." He nodded and then pretended he'd been struck by an idea. "I hear *California* is lovely this time of year..."

"Oh, you're *hilarious.*"

"I need you to investigate. It's probably nothing. Last time it was nothing."

"When was last time?"

He shrugged. "Forty years ago."

She clunked her head back against the headboard.

"I thought it was going to be *us* for a while."

He smiled.

"Absence makes the heart grow fonder."

Anne sighed.

"And who will I be watching?"

He closed his eyes and concentrated to recall the name.

There it is.

He opened his eyes.

"Catriona Phoenix."

~~ **THE END** ~~

WANT SOME MORE? FREE PREVIEWS!

If you liked this book, read on for a preview of the next Kilty AND the Shee McQueen Mystery-Thriller Series!

Thank you for reading! If you enjoyed this book, please swing back to Amazon and **leave me a review** — even short reviews help authors like me find new fans! You can also FOLLOW AMY on AMAZON

ENTER THE KILTY SWEEPSTAKES!

Enter the Kilty Sweepstakes for a chance to win a Kindle Reader and get free books! https://amyvansant.com/win-kindle-kilty

ABOUT THE AUTHOR

USA Today and Wall Street Journal bestselling author Amy Vansant has written over 20 books, including the fun, thrilling Shee McQueen series, the rollicking, twisty Pineapple Port Mysteries, and the action-packed Kilty urban fantasies. Throw in a couple of romances and a YA fantasy for her nieces...

Amy specializes in fun, exciting reads with plenty of laughs and action -- she tried to write serious books, but they always ended up full of jokes, so she gave up.

Amy lives in Jupiter, Florida with her muse/husband a goony Bordoodle named Archer.

BOOKS BY AMY VANSANT

Pineapple Port Mysteries
Funny, clean & full of unforgettable characters

Shee McQueen Mystery-Thrillers
Action-packed, fun romantic mystery-thrillers

Kilty Urban Fantasy/Romantic Suspense
Action-packed romantic suspense/urban fantasy

Slightly Romantic Comedies
Classic romantic romps

The Magicatory
Middle-grade fantasy

FREE PREVIEW

KILTY CONSCIENCE

CHAPTER ONE

Brochan watched her from a distance, her dark hair streaming behind her as she galloped across the glen upon a chestnut mare.

Like a princess from a fairytale.

Over her shoulder, she flashed a smile.

He urged on his mount.

Though he found himself fascinated with the other rider, their horses weren't fond of each other. His gelding nipped at her mare's neck when they rode side by side, so he'd fallen back.

What a happy accident to gain such a lovely view.

Reaching a lone oak, she reined in her horse and dismounted. He joined her, leaving his gelding on the opposite side of the great oak so the horses didn't antagonize one another. Both creatures dipped their heads to graze. No friends or foes when there was grass to be eaten.

The woman stared across the glen at Edinburgh castle, her back to him.

"We should return. People will blether," he said.

She glanced at him, the light in her eyes dancing with mischief. "You worry too much. No one saw us. And it's no matter. I'm from *America*. Here, they already think I'm *scandalous* for one reason or another."

He smiled and rested a hand on her hip, leaning close to whisper in her ear. "But it's mah duty tae protect yer honor."

She spun and placed her hands on his chest. "Then I have nothing to fear, do I?"

She tilted back her head and he kissed her. He couldn't not.

"Look whit ye made me dae," he said.

She slipped away from him, laughing. Patting her mare, she fussed with the bridle. "It's eighteen-thirty-three. Times are changing."

He frowned.

Eighteen-thirty-three?

That didn't seem right.

"Catriona, whit did ye say?"

He reached out to touch her shoulder and she faced him, scowling. "What did you call me?"

Something about her changed. He withdrew his hand and wiped his eyes. Refocusing, he saw her staring at him, but her features remained blurry.

"Somethin's wrong," he said.

She put her hands on her hips. "You know my name. Say it."

"Ah dinnae ken—"

"Say it."

He took a step back, a hissing sound building in his head.

"Say my *name*," she repeated stepping toward him. The light of the setting sun struck something in her hand and it flashed.

She was holding a knife.

Stumbling back, his heel struck the root of the oak and he fell against it. He put his hands on his ears as the growing din in his head roared like a storm-tossed ocean was trapped in his skull.

"Mah head. Somethin's wrong. Ah—"

He dropped to his knees.

She approached, standing over him.

"Say my name."

There has to be a way to make this noise stop.

"Say my name."

She was nearly upon him.

The noise became unbearable and he screamed.

"*Fiona!*"

Broch awoke sitting in a strange bed in an unfamiliar room. A low, snorty growl sounded beside him, and, recognizing it as a less-deafening version of the sound in his dream, he turned toward it.

In another bed, separated from his own by a small table, Catriona snored.

"Did you say something?"' she mumbled, her eyes fluttering open.

"Na," he said, laying back down.

She rolled over and her breathing grew heavy.

Broch remembered where they were. The drapes of their Tennessee hotel were drawn, but through the sliver where the fabric met, he saw it was still dark.

He whispered the name to himself to see how it felt on his tongue.

"*Fiona.*"

Get *Kilty Conscience* on Amazon!

ANOTHER FREE PREVIEW!

THE GIRL WHO WANTS

A Shee McQueen Mystery-Thriller by Amy Vansant

CHAPTER ONE

Three Weeks Ago, Nashua, New Hampshire.

Shee realized her mistake the moment her feet left the grass.

He's enormous.

She'd watched him drop from the side window of the house. He landed four feet from where she stood, and still, her brain refused to register the warning signs. The nose, big and lumpy as breadfruit, the forehead some beach town could use as a jetty if they buried him to his neck...

His knees bent to absorb his weight and *her* brain thought, *got you.*

Her brain couldn't be bothered with simple math: *Giant, plus Shee, equals Pain.*

Instead, she jumped to tackle him, dangling airborne as his knees straightened and the *pet the rabbit* bastard stood to his full height.

Crap.

The math added up pretty quickly after that.

Hovering like Superman mid-flight, there wasn't much she could do to change her disastrous trajectory. She'd *felt* like a superhero when she left the ground. Now, she felt more like a Canada goose staring into the propellers of Captain Sully's Airbus A320.

She might take down the plane, but it was going to *hurt.*

Frankenjerk turned toward her at the same moment she plowed into him. She clamped her arms around his waist like a little girl hugging a redwood. Lurch returned the embrace, twisting her to the ground. Her back hit the dirt and air burst from her lungs like a double shotgun blast.

Ow.

Wheezing, she punched upward, striking Beardless Hagrid in the throat.

That didn't go over well.

Grabbing her shoulder with one hand, Dickasaurus flipped her on her stomach like a sausage link, slipped his hand under her chin, and pressed his forearm against her windpipe.

The only air she'd gulped before he cut her supply stank of damp armpit. He'd tucked her cranium in his arm crotch, much like the famous noggin-less horseman once held his severed head. Fireworks exploded in the dark behind her eyes.

That's when a thought occurred to her.

I haven't been home in fifteen years.

What if she died in Gigantor's armpit? Would her father even know?

Has it been that long?

Flopping like a landed fish, she forced her assailant to adjust his hold and sucked a breath as she flipped on her back. Spittle glistened on his lips, his brow furrowed as if she'd asked him to read a paragraph of big-boy words.

His nostrils flared like the Holland Tunnel.

There's an idea.

Making a V with her fingers, Shee thrust upward, stabbing into his nose, straining to reach his tiny brain.

Goliath roared. Jerking back, he grabbed her arm to unplug her fingers from his nose socket. She whipped away her limb before he had a good grip, fearing he'd snap her bones with his Godzilla paws.

Kneeling before her, he clamped both hands over his face, cursing as blood seeped from behind his fingers.

Shee's gaze didn't linger on that mess. Her focus fell to his crotch, hovering a foot above her feet, protected by nothing but a thin pair of oversized sweatpants.

Scrambled eggs, sir?

She kicked.

He howled.

Shee scuttled back like a crab, found her feet, and snatched her gun from her side. The gun she should have pulled *before* trying to tackle the Empire State Building.

"Move a muscle and I'll aerate you," she said. She always liked that line.

The golem growled, but remained on the ground like a good dog, cradling his family jewels.

Shee's partner in this manhunt, a local cop easier on the eyes than he was useful, rounded the corner and drew his weapon.

She smiled and holstered the gun he'd lent her. Unknowingly.

"Glad you could make it."

Her portion of the operation accomplished, she headed toward the car as more officers swarmed the scene.

"Shee, where are you going?" called the cop.

She stopped and turned.

"Home, I think."

His gaze dropped to her hip.

"Is that my gun?"

Get *The Girl Who Wants* on Amazon!

ISBN-10: 1541356179

ISBN-10: 9781541356177

Library of Congress: 2016921498

Vansant Creations, LLC / Amy Vansant
Jupiter, FL
http://www.AmyVansant.com

Copy editing by Carolyn Steele

Proofreading by Effrosyni Moschoudi, Meg Barnhart & Connie Leap

Cover by Lance Buckley & Amy Vansant